IN THE SHADOWS OF THE WORKHOUSE

ANNIE SHIELDS

PROLOGUE

*S*hropshire
1866

JOHN COBB WAITED for the second knock at the front door before he set his book down, abandoning his spot next to the roaring fire.

He'd seen them coming up the driveway, of course. Storms like the one lashing the building usually caused the rats to desert the sinking ship. He could hardly miss the lone woman clutching blankets to her chest as she dragged along the small child behind her.

He took his time putting on his overcoat. The woman wasn't going anywhere, not with the storm raging overhead.

He straightened his cravat and ran a hand over his hair. As the Porter at Brookford workhouse, he had a certain image to uphold, even in the dead of night.

He yanked open the door, casting his beady eyes over the bedraggled form of the woman and her daughter. Rain splattered in through the open space as the wind roared overhead, making him squint. His gaze settled on the blankets she clutched to her chest. Not blankets, he amended, just another hungry mouth to feed.

"What?"

"Please, sir," the woman stammered, her words garbled by fear as much as cold. Rainwater ran in rivulets down her face, plastering her hair to her head, and dripping from the hem of her soaked dress. "My children and I... we need outdoor relief. Please, sir, have a heart, we need –"

Cobb pushed the door open with an irritated sigh and held his lamp aloft for a closer look. She didn't look as malnourished as some who came knocking at his door. He'd wager her dress was better quality than most when she was dry. It was rare that he had a woman of means calling at his door, especially one as attractive as this one. Most people were emaciated and dressed in rags, knowing that they had no other options left but the workhouse.

"Outdoor relief, you say? Where are you from?"

"I am on my way south," the woman said quickly, her teeth chattering. "We got caught in the storm. I just need a bed for the night. I will be on my way in the morning. I am going to meet family, to seek financial support because my husband…"

"Where is your parish?"

"I'm from Chorley," the woman explained.

"Then go to your own bloody parish and ask them to feed you and your bastards." John started to close the door, but the woman placed a hand on it. "I am begging you, sir, have mercy. We are soaked through. My infant has been quiet for the past few hours, and I fear that something might be terribly wrong. Do you by chance have a medical officer you can call upon?"

John Cobb made a face. He found himself wondering what she would look like in dry clothes. And he remembered what the master had said about needing young, healthy people. She looked to be in her twenties, and healthy enough if you had a penchant for drowned rats. But there was the issue of the children. He debated, wondering what the Master would want to do about them.

"One night, you say?"

"Yes," the woman said quickly. "I will be on my way in the morning. I just need to rest somewhere dry. I am on my way to–"

"I don't need your family history," John Cobb snapped. He pushed the door open so the woman and her children could step in. She had a cloth sack tied across her back, and the young girl next to her had a similar one. He imagined those bags contained all their worldly possessions. "You can leave your bags in here," he said as he turned the key in the lock and slipped it into his pocket.

"But why? These are all that I carried from the home I had with my husband."

"This is the workhouse," John Cobb retorted, his patience wearing thin. "You can only seek relief if you have nothing. Leave your bloody things on the side and stop dripping on my damn floor."

The child pressed herself closer to her mother's soaked skirts. Big, dark eyes stared up fearfully at him.

"Sir, please, mind your language in front of my daughter."

John Cobb stared at the young woman trembling before him. There was a determined light in her eyes, and he felt lust pool in his loins. He did like it when a woman had a bit of spirit. He grinned at her and was rewarded when she shrank further away from him.

"Welcome to the Brookford workhouse. Let me show you where you'll be staying tonight."

CHAPTER 1

 rookford Workhouse
Shropshire, 1881

THE CHILL of the stone floor seeped into the fabric of her ugly workhouse dress as Maisie Milne sat hunched in the corner of the broom cupboard. She adjusted her position in the cramped space, her inert muscles protesting painfully. Somewhere in the darkness, her movement set up a scurrying sound and she swallowed a scream as something warm and furry ran across her legs.

She sighed softly, leaning her head against the coarse brick wall. The scent of old straw brooms and dust was almost comforting in its familiarity.

Still, confinement in here was preferable to being sent to the Refractory Ward or locked in the laundry room on a boiling hot summer's day. She couldn't tell if it was merely hours or a few days that had passed when she heard footsteps approaching. She didn't have much time to ready herself for whatever came next. The door rattled as it was unlocked and it creaked open, filling her dark prison with blinding light.

The stern figure of Mrs Pursley, the matron of Brookford Workhouse, loomed in the entry, her hawkish eyes narrowing as they fell upon Maisie's shivering form.

"Are you ready to come out and repent, girl?" she demanded, her voice as cold and hard as the stone floors of the workhouse.

In her heart, a tiny flame of defiance flickered, and Maisie wanted nothing more than to tell the old trout exactly what she could do with her repentance, but years of experience had taught her the harsh rules of the workhouse. Survival here meant contrition, a game of shadows and masks she had learned to play all too well.

She swallowed hard and replied, "Yes, Matron. I am ready."

The Matron watched the girl struggling to stand before she reached in and hauled Maisie up. Maisie squinted when she was set roughly on her feet in the corridor, lifting a hand to shield her eyes. A hand that was then swatted away, leaving Maisie to screw up her face as her eyes adjusted to the light change. The broom cupboard was at the end of the long hall, adjacent to the scullery and the storeroom, culminating in the kitchen at one end where women worked throughout the day to provide food for the inmates of the workhouse.

The smell of bland stew, meagre in its content yet tantalising to her starved senses, drifted from the large cast-iron pots to tease her ravenous belly.

"Well?" Mrs Pursley prodded her with a sharp finger. "What do you have to say to me? And make sure you mean it, Maisie Milne, else you'll be back in there faster than you can say Jack Robinson."

Maisie tucked her head into her chest, well-practised in the art of apologising. She'd stepped under the cane meant for Daft Janey, trying to protect the older woman from one of Matron's beatings simply because poor Janey couldn't follow lots of instructions at once. The inmates knew this and so only gave Daft Janey simple tasks one at a time to keep her from making a mistake. Mrs Pursley was still new at the work-house and Maisie had tried to intervene in the beating to explain how to get Daft Janey to do the work.

"I'm sorry that I called you bad names, Mrs

Pursley," Maisie began. "And that I tried to tell you how to do your job."

The woman's sharp inhale of breath drew Maisie's gaze upwards briefly before it dropped to the ground again. The battleaxe's face twisted as if she'd stepped in something unpleasant. Maisie pushed away the memory of Mrs Pursley's horrified expression when she'd called her a harridan to her face, lest her lips twitch in glee.

"I am but an orphan, Mrs Pursley," she said in her best mournful tone. "A stupid orphan who forgot her place. I am sorry. It won't happen again."

Her contrite acknowledgement was rewarded with a stern nod, and soon she found herself being ushered into the dining room, amidst a sea of other similarly clad children. Row upon row of benches were filled. They all sat in forced silence, their heads bowed in quiet prayers over steaming bowls, the only sound being the faint clatter of cutlery and the rustle of shuffling bodies.

Maisie felt the weight of their attention as she collected her bowl and grimy spoon. She waited for her rations; a bowl of stew that held more water than meat, and a few white lumps that might have once been a vegetable. She had a slice of bread that must have been a few days old as it was stiff. At least it would soften up in the brown water. She passed by the scales, not daring to ask for the ration size to be checked. They all knew the scales were only there for show in case the workhouse was inspected. She took her place on a long, hard bench and bowed her head.

Although conversation was forbidden, over the years the children had learned to communicate in hushed tones barely audible over the scraping of spoons against bowls, a secret language born out of necessity and camaraderie. From these whispers, Maisie learned that Daft Janey was fine. Her beating had been forgotten in the sudden chaos when Maisie had stepped in to intervene. That small piece of good news filled her with relief, and she finished her meal with relish.

Emerging into the chilly expanse of the outdoor women's yard, Maisie filled her lungs with the crisp, fresh air that revived her senses after being shut in the broom cupboard for so long. Spring was in the air, but the steel sky promised rain. Her breath formed a thin cloud in front of her.

All around her, mothers and children came together in bittersweet reunions, their joyous sobs echoing off the high walls of the yard. It was a precious window of time when the harsh rules were softened, the only occasion in their gruelling day when mothers were allowed the chance to hold their children close. The sight stirred a yearning within Maisie, filling her with wistful thoughts of her own mother. Would she have blanketed her face with tender kisses, she wondered, or perhaps, given the chance, she would have been able to arrange their discharge from this place. Under different circumstances, Maisie might have never seen the inside of the broom cupboard or felt the wrath of Matron's birch cane at all.

Maisie's gaze drifted across to where other women were staring up at the windows of the men's day room. There, she could see men with a hand pressed to the inside of the glass, staring down at the families that they could see yet remained out of reach because of the workhouse rules separating husbands from wives, able-bodied from infirm, and children from families. Some women waved tattered rags in a quiet greeting to their loved ones whilst others openly cried.

Maisie pulled her gaze from the harrowing scenes.

The children who didn't have families here had grabbed up the shabby wooden toys; a cup and ball, or a hoop and stick to entertain themselves. She watched from afar, a reluctant smile tugging on her lips. For some, they found pure joy in jostling with their friends, immune to the chill that must be biting painfully at their bare feet. Still, dancing around in the damp air, even momentarily, was a most welcome change to being inside. Maisie had to wrap her arms around her middle to ward off the cold when she felt two hands cover her eyes.

She grabbed at the hands, fear turning her fingers into claws until a familiar voice murmured into her ear, "Guess who?"

CHAPTER 2

"*D*uncan!"

With his familiar lanky form towering over her, Duncan Burke was indeed a sight for sore eyes. His light brown hair and eyes the colour of cornflowers in a summer meadow, set her heart fluttering. He'd grown since the last time she'd laid eyes on him – taller, broader, and she saw the whiskers on his cheeks. Her initial delight at seeing her good friend swiftly gave way to niggling concern. She hadn't expected to see him here until the leaves began to turn, signalling the end of the harvest season. His presence here, in the middle of April, furrowed her brows.

Their friendship had been cemented within these forbidding walls, built during the cyclical routine of Duncan and his family entering the workhouse each winter. His usually vibrant eyes were now shadowed with grief, his mouth set in a firm, sombre line. The sight of him, so defeated, was like a punch to her gut.

"What's happened?" she asked.

"My father..." He said quietly, his eyes not meeting hers. "He was tilling. There was an accident. The wagon... Father fell over the back. We think the horses got startled... the plough..." He paused, his tortured gaze sweeping the walled yard, though she didn't think he truly saw the skinny children playing there.

He didn't need to explain further. Years of living in a workhouse that serviced such a rural area had conditioned her to hear tales of tragic accidents on farms. She could only imagine William Burke ending up beneath the merciless blades of a plough.

"Duncan, I... I'm so sorry," she said, reaching out to squeeze his hand.

"Ma, she didn't last long after that. I think... I think she died of a broken heart."

She blinked back tears, threatening to spill over. Mary Burke was a sweet soul. His parents were a couple who had embraced a humble life, desiring little more than to feed their family with the fruits of their labour. But the relentless demands of farming life, coupled with the unpredictability of the seasons, had them teetering on the edge of poverty, the workhouse doors opening for them more often than not.

She could see the grief etched on his young face, the light in his eyes dimmed by tragedy. With no family to protect him and no means of income, he had ended up back in here.

"I wish there was something I could do to make things easier for you," she murmured. The depth of his loss resonated within her, echoing like a stone dropping into a deep well. Like her, Duncan was now an orphan. His siblings had all succumbed to the harshness of their existence during their childhood, leaving him alone in this world.

Absentmindedly, Duncan reached out to touch her hair and removed a cobweb, a soft smile tugging at the corners of his mouth. "And who were you sticking up for to end up in the broom cupboard this time, Maisie Milne?" he asked, his tone gentle, seeking comfort in their familiar banter.

His question drew a watery chuckle from Maisie. "You know me, I love that broom cupboard so much, I think I should just live in there."

"With just the spiders and mice for company, no doubt," Duncan replied.

Maisie's heart squeezed a little when she

realised that he was making light of the situation despite his world having irrevocably changed.

"You could come visit me there, though there wouldn't be much room for you. Have you been sleeping in the manure pile, Duncan Burke? You've filled out!" She clapped him on the shoulder and was rewarded with his light laugh.

Self-consciously, Duncan lifted a shoulder and his cheeks reddened endearingly. He looked down at the workhouse union clothing. He wore the union-issued trousers and a heavy calico shirt, with the cloth hat perching jauntily on his head. Each person entering the workhouse had to surrender all property, including their clothing that was taken away for disinfection and then stored until the person was ready to leave. The rough Fearnought cloth was durable, true enough, but she knew that Duncan hated what it represented; that his family's dreams of leasing land had failed again. "My mother said that I must take after her brother, being so tall already."

"You'll be in the men's yard before you know it. Lord knows you stick out like a sore thumb in here with us children."

Duncan tilted his head, a brow arched. "We're the same age, Maisie. You'll be in the women's yard yourself before long, too."

Maisie was dreading moving from the children's part into the women's section. Some of the stories she'd heard about what happened there sent tremors of unease coursing through her, though she was determined not to let her worry show through.

"John Cobb was still as mean as ever when I was standing there with the union official seeking indoor relief. I tried to tell them I could work the land, but they insisted I'm still too young."

"You will be apprenticed out soon enough, Duncan. Make no mistake about that."

His expression was riddled with disbelief, and she tried not to take it to heart. He'd lost everything and it would be hard to remain upbeat considering what he'd been through.

"Tell me what other news you learned out there?"

Maisie had lived in the workhouse most of her life. She had almost no memory of the world beyond the hefty stone walls, other than the lanes away from the workhouse that led to the local village and the churchyard that she had only walked along behind a coffin when attending a pauper's burial.

"Much the same subject as in here, I expect," he said. "The death of the master's wife in someone so young and so… suspicious."

Maisie frowned. "Suspicious? She fell down the

stairs in the dead of the night. Hardly surprising considering how steep the stairs are up to the second floor."

"I'm just repeating local gossip," he answered. "The workhouse has been home to many of them. It shouldn't be too surprising that Mr Finnegan isn't all that liked, should it?"

"I suppose not," Maisie replied. Edith Finnegan had been a stern woman, as cold as her husband without an ounce of warmth for the unfortunate souls that she lived with. Maisie couldn't see how her losing her balance in the dead of the night and being found at the foot of the stairs earlier that year was suspicious, though.

"What news in here?"

This time, Maisie snorted her derision. "The same as ever. Up at a quarter to six, breakfast at half past, and begin work for seven. Finish work at six in the evening and bed for eight. Nothing changes in here except for the weather," she finished.

"What about the new Matron? What's her name?"

"Mrs Pursley," Maisie supplied, keeping her voice low so she wouldn't be overheard. "She's about as warm as a December day and just as pleasant as having a rat in the bed."

"I heard a rumour that a new schoolteacher is starting?"

Maisie's attention snapped to him. For as long as she could remember, Mrs Finnegan had taught the children of Brookford workhouse. For three hours every day, they'd sat in the schoolroom, sometimes shivering at their plain wooden desks as ice covered the inside of the windows, as she had recited her letters dutifully. "Do you think that's true?"

Duncan shrugged. "Anyone with eyes could tell that Mrs Finnegan hated teaching. Has the new Matron given any schooling?"

Maisie shook her head. "We've had nothing for weeks, ever since Mr Park disappeared."

Unlike most of the other children, Maisie was keen to learn. She knew some of the older women who'd learned to read and to write, and that it had given them the means to work. She wanted to be apprenticed out into service as soon as she was old enough. She had plans to do anything to stay out of the workhouse once she was able to leave.

But the finicky Mr Park, with his natty suit and wire spectacles, didn't seem to want to allow his students to dream beyond these walls. The school-master had been miserly and stern, though he'd not raised his hand to the children once.

"Matron told Tilly Evans when she asked about

it that girls like us didn't have to know how to read, only how to pick oakum."

"I dare say that hasn't gone down too well with the board of guardians. Perhaps that's why they've decided to hire another teacher. Let's hope that whoever they hire is a better person than the staff we've got," He pointed to the tell-tale red lines that spanned her thin wrists. "I can tell you're already acquainted with the new Matron's cane. What happened?"

She followed his lead, distracting him with tales of the other inmates and the recent happenings within the workhouse. Before long, Matron called the children in. Maisie tried to close off hearing the cries and woeful sounds of mothers being separated from their offspring once more. Duncan must have noticed her discomfort, for he reached for her hand and gave her a reassuring smile. Together, they stepped inside the workhouse, their alliance the one thing that gave her comfort. Duncan had suffered such a sad loss but having him back again so soon allowed Maisie to feel hopeful for the summer.

CHAPTER 3

"I'm sure that your role and responsibilities as schoolmistress here at Brookford were outlined by the Guardians at your interview," Mrs Pursley explained briskly.

Portia Summerhill nodded, swapping her carpet bag to her other hand. "Yes, they were quite detailed."

The interview had been held at the village Rectory. The board of guardians had been thorough in questioning her experience and her training before offering her the schoolteacher position. To her, they'd all seemed to be more concerned about spending twenty-five pounds a year out of their budget on her salary than whether she was qualified for the role.

Portia had to remind herself that this was her

new beginning. Still, as she'd made her way along the thin drive that was lined with tall Poplars and nasturtiums, looking upon the formidable façade of the workhouse in the low morning light, she was filled with anxiety.

Nestled among the rolling green hills and the ancient forests of oak and sycamore, Brookford Workhouse served fifty-two of the local parishes. It was a mammoth edifice, austere in its design with a red-brick facade that spoke of the hard realities contained within its walls. The structure was built to a precise square plan, its architecture more akin to a prison than a refuge.

"I'm quite sure that they were," the Matron huffed as she led Portia through a heavy wooden door that she closed and then locked behind them, the keys on the big iron ring rattling ominously. Portia felt a chill settle over her. Not from the dank morning air, but from the stark reality of the place that was now her home. "But just in case they missed anything, I've been asked by the master to go over things with you. As matron, I am in charge of the women inmates. You are to oversee the children, including their schooling."

"Isn't it unusual that there's a matron as well as a schoolmistress here?"

Matron Pursley stopped, peering at her carefully and Portia could see the indignation shining back at her. "We have capacity for one hundred and fifty inmates here. We are connected to over fifty local parishes throughout the county. Currently, we have two hundred and seven souls under this roof. I told the Master that I needed help. That I couldn't do it all alone."

Portia made an appropriate sound of pity. "That's a lot of work for one person, Mrs Pursley."

The Matron stared hard at her for another moment or two before she continued as though Portia hadn't interrupted her. "No less than three hours of education a day. If the children are attending church, you must accompany them. You are up at six in the morning, and your day ends at eight in the evening when bedtime is." Matron paused again, a look of distaste twisting her mouth.

"Your food rations and candles are all part of your wage, and you are not permitted to leave the site unless you have express permission from the master and the guardians. That one," Mrs Pursley's sharp tone and extended index finger indicated its importance, "is what tripped up our last Schoolmaster."

Portia Summerhill tried to quell the jitteriness churning her breakfast and exhaled quietly. "I understand."

Matron rattled off the daily routine – no Sundays off around here – leading her along a maze of corridors and narrow stone staircases. She was shown out into the yard, and she inhaled sharply, trying to rid her lungs of the stale air that seemed to permeate her senses already.

Everything within the grounds was encircled by a looming stone wall that stood twelve feet high, an ever-present boundary that separated the worlds of those who had, and those who had nothing.

Matron led her through an arch. Separate from the main structure and concealed behind it, stood the infirmary and refractory wards that butted up against the perimeter buildings. She pointed out various doors, naming the washhouse, slaughterhouse, piggery, laundry room, and bakehouse, as well as a multitude of storage rooms for potatoes, coal, and flour which were built into what formed the border of the workhouse. Whatever was produced here at the workhouse was used to feed the inmates as well as being sold to make money to pay for the upkeep of the building and the inmates.

Beyond the oppressive wall, a series of sheds and stables sprawled across the land. These structures served as a haven for the few who were fortunate enough to be assigned to the care of the workhouse's livestock, a task that provided a brief respite from the relentless drudgery within the workhouse walls. Portia tried not to stare at the people as they went about their work, all dressed in the same coarse brown cloth, the union-issued uniforms that identified them as workhouse inmates if they were to venture into the local villages.

Matron steered them back towards the main building. Portia looked up at the frontage, at the blank iron-framed windows that were like soulless eyes staring out across the idyllic countryside that it sat in, and she shuddered. She had to remind herself that she was no stranger to hard work or adversity. The stakes of this undertaking might be high, but she was resolved to see it through.

She had to pull her thoughts back to what Matron was telling her. She needed to pay attention and stay focused. She couldn't lose her nerve now. She walked behind Matron along the stony path towards the porter's room where people seeking both indoor and outdoor relief would be greeted by Mr Cobb. The door swung open like the maws of a dragon awaiting its next victim, though the porter was absent from his post. Mrs Pursley explained it away because the porter had had a late night, no doubt tending to his work. Behind the porter's room was the waiting room; a plain room with a bench against a wall and a hearth that remained cold and unlit.

At the centre of the building was an octagonal hub. This nexus housed the master's quarters, positioned so that he could cast an ever-watchful eye upon the daily toil and turmoil of the inmates. No doubt, his gaze was a constant reminder of the power he wielded.

Flanking the octagonal hub were two-story accommodation wings. These were the dormitories, the sleeping quarters for the many who called the workhouse their home, though they were far from the warmth and comfort a home should provide.

"The master indicated that you are not a local girl."

"I'm from Berkshire, though I grew up not far from here. My aunt Rosamund ensured I received a good education. She held firm in the belief that education was the pathway to enlightenment."

Mrs Pursley's mouth pinched white. "You ought to wait until you've met some of your young inmates before offering them enlightenment, Miss Summerhill."

"They're children, Mrs Pursley. All in need of nurturing."

The matron's reaction was a scoff, her jowly face folding into a sour expression. "You have got an idealistic nature, Miss Summerhill," she retorted. "The workhouse will soon squeeze that nonsense right out of you."

Portia clenched her jaw but remained steadfast.

ANNIE SHIELDS

"I've taken on this role with a full understanding of the challenges, Matron Pursley. I hope to elevate these children's lives. Education transformed my life, and I intend to do the same for them."

Matron Pursley squinted at her, her lips pursed in a tight line, the lines around her mouth deepening. "You're wasting your time with these wretches," she said in a dismissive tone. "Many of the people here... they're a drain on society. They can't work or won't work. Education won't change that."

"Perhaps," Portia replied evenly, her determination hardening. She'd been ready for these comments, but it was still difficult to hold her tongue.

The matron continued her tirade as she led Portia deeper into the workhouse. "It's hard enough trying to maintain order in this place. The inmates are forever complaining, 'I'm hungry,' or 'I'm cold.' As if they're the only ones who are suffering. As if we're not doing our best to keep them alive. They never do as they're told. They think they're hard done by when it's folks like me, the hard-working people of this land, who facilitate their lives. Ungrateful lot!"

Portia walked along the hollow halls, up an uneven stone staircase. She listened, heard the bitterness in the other woman's tone and it made

26

her heart ache, to hear so many souls dismissed as worthless. Was she ready for this fight?

"Everyone deserves a chance at betterment, Matron," she said, her voice echoing slightly in the stone corridor.

The eye roll and accompanying snort were rife with derision. "They've all got the devil in them. Mark my words. Now," she turned and headed for the door, her back signalling the end of that particular subject. "In the future, you are to use the back door. The main entrance is reserved for the Master and the Porter, and any languisher seeking relief only." She held open the door for Portia and made a gesture that she steps through it, adding, "Staff go around the back."

Portia tried to smile though the woman didn't soften in the least. "Where is the Master of the Workhouse? I had hoped to meet him, seeing as he was absent from the interview process."

"The master is a busy man," Mrs Pursley allowed the door to slam shut behind them though her tone softened for the first time. "He has a lot on his plate since the sad passing of his wife earlier this year. It was so sudden, so unexpected."

"She was the matron here, wasn't she?"

"Yes. I'm not one for gossip and I shan't thank you for speaking about such a thing in front of the master or the inmates. Mr Finnegan was recommended by his mentor and guardian for the work-house, Reverend James.

He has been the master here at Brookford for more than a decade. He is to be commended, being appointed at such a young age to an important position. Mrs Finnegan was hired on as matron not long after he became master here, and they quickly fell in love. Mrs Finnegan was older than he. God-fearing but not the friendliest, so I'm told."

Mrs Pursley sounded proud of this fact and Portia had to keep the smile off her face. "Is that so?"

"It is," Mrs Pursley nodded emphatically. "I never did see a man so churned up by grief and yet he's kept a head on his shoulders, trying his best for the sake of all the people under his care. He's a good man. A good man burdened by his heartache. Yet, even though he's heartbroken, he hasn't devi-ated from his work once."

"How very sad for the master," Portia said quietly as she stepped through the door. She waited until the matron had locked the door before asking, "How did she pass?"

"What did I say about nefarious gossip?" The snippy tone was back.

Portia had already heard the talk about the unexpected loss of Mrs Finnegan and how she'd been discovered at the foot of a staircase with a broken neck and a candle on the floor next to her. She apologised for the question as she briefly wondered which staircase it was and if she could avoid it.

Any further talk halted when they reached the end of the corridor on the top floor which had an offshoot of doors that splayed out on either side. Mrs Pursley pushed open the one on the left and ushered Portia through it.

"Here we are," Matron dropped a set of keys onto the mahogany tallboy next to the door. "This is your room."

The room was bright and airy, with sturdy furniture and a wide bed with a canopy. Immediately, she was struck by the differences between where the light that poured through the windows and the whitewashed walls, compared to the dreary grey floors below them.

The wall on the right was dominated by a large fireplace, with a brass coal scuttle and poker sitting on the wide hearth. She had an empty bookcase and a bedside table, with a cherrywood desk under the windowsill of one of the windows. Portia kept her face passive as she walked to the window. Green verdant hills rolled away into the distance, with the tiled rooftops of the nearby village peeking out of the emerald canopy of trees.

"I imagine it's not up to your standards but–"

"It's fine," Portia said briskly. Memories of times gone by, of cramped spaces and smelly bodies crushed into the same bed, shimmered at the periphery of her mind. The matron's brows raised at the tart tone and Portia forced her mouth into a smile that she was far from feeling. "Thank you for taking the time to show me around, Mrs Pursley. I know that you have much more important things to do with your day. I can take it from here."

For a moment, Portia thought that the matron was about to argue but she must have decided against it. "You have the day to settle in. During the summer months, our day starts at half past five. Half six in the winter."

Portia nodded, thanked the woman again and waited for the door to close before she made her shoulders relax. Her gaze travelled around the room.

A voice in her head impatiently urged her to run away. She shut it off and set her bag on the foot of the bed. She'd deliberately kept her belongings to a minimum, leaving behind all her fine dresses and jewellery. She had achieved the first part of her plan. Despite the matron's discouraging words, Portia's determination was unshaken. Armed with nothing but her conviction, she was ready to brave the fight ahead.

CHAPTER 4

The familiar clatter and warmth of the Brookford Workhouse kitchen was a welcome haven for Maisie Milne.

The room was filled with workers. Huge pots and copper urns sat bubbling away on the colossal black range that filled the alcove on one side. Pans and kitchen utensils hung from the roof. A row of butler sinks were tucked under the windows and three long oak tables occupied much of the red-tiled floor space, each area filled with inmates working diligently to feed their comrades.

Maisie had gladly accepted the kitchen tasks handed out by Matron that morning because it meant a day away from the oakum picking, even if it made her clothing itchier as she sweated in the humid room. There was an unwritten rule that those who worked in the kitchen could pilfer a bit more food. Maisie would be sure to pocket what she could when the cook wasn't looking. The extra morsels she stole always found their way to the sickly young ones; their wide-eyed gratitude more satisfying than the stolen food itself.

Across the vast kitchen, Joan Wilson, the elderly cook, ruled with an iron spoon. Formerly of a grand local estate, her lack of family had landed her here at Brookford Workhouse at the end of her working life.

Classed as infirm because of their age, most women in their twilight years sat in the corner of the yard, knitting or weaving quietly. Mrs Wilson refused to accept such an unfavourable label. She would tell anyone who'd listen to her that she'd been able-bodied since she could walk, and then she'd get right back to work. Maisie would wager that Joan Wilson would make even Mrs Pursley tremble in her boots. Her brisk, no-nonsense manner set the rhythm of the kitchen, creating an impression of what it might have been like to serve under her in grander circumstances.

Maisie followed orders, darting about the wide kitchen with practised ease. Most days, dinner would comprise of mutton or beef stew, and a slice of bread. They would prepare a treacle tart or suet pudding with the understanding that it was only for the staff of the workhouse and not the inmates.

The new inmate, Nellie Jones, was hunched over a bucket, peeling potatoes with a faraway look in her bright green eyes. Her raven black hair contrasted strikingly with her rosy complexion, flushed from the steam of the boiling pots.

"Those potatoes won't peel themselves, my girl," Joan Wilson barked gruffly, a wary eye on the door. "Just because you're new, that don't mean that you get a free pass on slacking with your work. Matron's due any minute and we can't be running behind."

Nellie shook her head and rolled her eyes. "Keep yer knickers on! They'll get done."

Maisie skirted around the edge of the pair, all too aware of how quickly Joan could wield that spoon.

"I want the stew done this side of Christmas!"

Nellie nonchalantly dropped a potato into the bucket and took her time reaching into the muslin sack for another.

Another kitchen inmate, Ethel Crabtree, chimed in. "We'll not get supper if we haven't done our tasks, Nellie. That means we'll all go hungry. Mrs Pursley runs a tight ship. Best not cross her."

"I don't know about you but this slop you're all

---

so excited about can't be termed as a stew," Nellie smirked.

Joan Wilson exploded. "I won't be going without supper because of your laziness, Nellie Jones! Now, take your thick head out of the clouds and get peeling!"

Maisie was curious about the newcomer. Most new inmates were fearful and ashamed. Nellie had taken indoor relief with her small child. It was rare for a single mother to enter Brookford; most seemed to abandon their children at the door instead.

But Nellie seemed eerily content for someone who'd just been confined, her cheerful demeanour prompting Ethel to demand, "Why are you looking so pleased with yourself? This isn't a pleasure house, it's a workhouse."

Nellie looked up then. "Maybe I've got a reason to be cheerful," she said cryptically, her eyes sparkling.

"You're new around here, so you don't know the rules. You don't want to be on the end of Matron's birch cane. Trust me on that," Ethel said.

Nellie, unimpressed, merely shrugged. "Matron won't touch me. Mr Cobb wouldn't like that."

Cook scoffed loudly. "John Cobb? The Porter?"

"That's right," Nellie said, a smug smile curving her full lips.

"That man wouldn't give two hoots what happens to you."

Nellie, aghast at such an accusation, glared at Joan. "That's not true! He's a kind man. Sweet and good."

Ethel fisted her hands on her bony hips, confused. "John Cobb doesn't have a caring bone in his body. You'd do well to stay out of his way, too. You won't be the first pretty girl that he's taken a shine to. Bad things happen to women that he sets his sights on."

"Nonsense," Nellie grumbled. "He said that people don't understand him. If he was as bad as you all say, why did he give me a slice of cherry pie when I arrived? He even fetched a bottle for my bairn. Now, tell me that isn't a kind gesture for a woman down on her luck?"

A stunned silence filled the kitchen, the women glancing at each other, their minds racing back to their own harsh encounters with John Cobb.

Maisie hardly thought of the night that she'd arrived at the workhouse. Thinking about such things was a waste of time. Her mother had died. That was that. She couldn't recall what her mother looked like, nor the sound of her voice. She just remembered waking the next morning and her mother not being next to her. She'd never seen her again.

A memory teased Maisie and she frowned, trying to reach into the recesses of her mind but it evaporated like steam in front of her. No matter how hard she tried to draw on it, it wouldn't come clear. Instead, the mutterings about the Porter fluttered over her head.

John Cobb was cold and unfeeling. He was cruel and mean. The inmates here believed that the very thought of having to face him upon entering the place was what kept most people out of the workhouse. Only the very desperate would risk a run-in with him. The fleeting images that shimmered at the edges of her mind vanished when Daisy came bursting into the kitchen, hissing that Matron was on her way. The news was enough to get the kitchen back into motion in time for when the door opened, and Mrs Pursley walked in to inspect their morning's labours.

Maisie had to wait until later in the afternoon when the mothers and children were mingling, before she had the opportunity to speak to Duncan alone. She spotted him easily, his long-limbed frame placing him head and shoulders above the rest. When he met her gaze with a smile, her heart gave a little leap of joy. She knew that he still grieved the loss of his family, but he'd settled easily back into the routine of the workhouse. She looked forward to their daily chats, and she found herself willing for the hours of the day to go by faster so that she could get into the yard to see him. It had always been this way, only now the sun was shining, and they weren't huddled together for warmth during the winter months. But she also knew that he was biding his time until he could leave Brookford. He wanted to work the land, just as his family had done. Hearing him talk about life beyond the walls also fuelled a desire in her to leave here but she didn't dare ask him if she would be included in the life that he imagined for himself.

She had saved him a slice of bread and, as he ate half of it, she relayed the story of Nellie Jones and her surprising endorsement of John Cobb.

Maisie didn't miss how he'd tucked the other half of the bread into the pocket of his breeches, no doubt having someone in mind to share the extra ration with. Duncan was ever the generous soul.

"Do you think it's true, what people are saying about him?" he asked when she had finished her tale.

"In all honesty, I've never had much to do with him. I barely remember the night I arrived here," she confessed, "although…"

"Although what?"

She tried delving into her memory again and drew a blank as to what that image was. She shook her head. "It's nothing."

Duncan cocked a brow, and Maisie blushed over the lie. "Come on, out with it?"

She sighed. "You'll think I'm silly but earlier in the kitchen, when Nellie was talking about Mr Cobb sharing a piece of pie, I could have sworn there was a memory there, but it's gone."

Duncan touched her arm in concern, and she drew comfort from his touch. "From the night you were taken into Brookford?"

Maisie shrugged. "I don't know. Perhaps."

It pained her, not to have that memory. It was old Mrs Harp, one of the older inmates who'd passed some time ago, who'd told her that she'd been four years old when she'd been admitted to the workhouse. But she'd been alone.

Despite Maisie's adamant claims of having someone with her, every inmate present on the morning she awoke in a dirty, unfamiliar bed among strangers insisted that she had been abandoned at the front door or that her mother had passed away the night they arrived. Regardless of claims made by them all, Maisie was confident that she'd not been alone that night when she'd walked up the stony path to the front door. But her memories were hazy, faceless shapes. Maisie wished with all her heart that she had a memory of her mother. Just one image to hold on to in the dark.

She scrubbed at her face, the skin on her palms

rough and tender. "All I know is the women here don't like him, and that's good enough for me."

Duncan, who'd finished with his morsel of bread, followed Maisie's line of sight to where Nellie Jones was dancing in the corner, laughing gaily with a small boy in her arms. The woman's dark locks bounced down her back, her workhouse cloth cap balancing at a jaunty angle on the back of her head. "She doesn't act like she's in the workhouse, does she?" he asked with a hint of disbelief in his voice.

"Maybe that's the key to survival in here," Maisie said. "To grab each moment of happiness with both hands, even the hand of a rotter like John Cobb, and to live each day as if it's your last."

CHAPTER 5

ortia Summerhill grasped the doorknob of the workhouse master's parlour and inhaled a breath, letting it out slowly through her lips to try and steady her thundering heart, before she pushed the door open with a determined force.

"Ah, there you are, Miss Summerhill," Mrs Draper said. Her voice, soft yet persistent, cut through the murmur of the room. A petite woman, she reminded Portia of a nervous sparrow, constantly in motion; her slender fingers were forever adjusting her shawl or patting her bonnet into place. Portia knew her to be a spinster who'd inherited a considerable sum of money. She was unusual in her position as there weren't many women who were accepted onto a board of guardians despite the laws changing some years ago.

The selection process of the board was fairly straightforward. A vacancy had to present itself first before an interested party could offer their services to the workhouse master. Their eligibility then hinged on the decision of the current board members. Local entrepreneurs often exploited this opening to advance their own interests, embedding themselves within the workhouse structure. The board, responsible for the governance of more than fifty parishes, was composed of over forty guardians. However, not every member felt obliged to attend regularly, and some, indeed, never made an appearance.

Portia's gaze swept the room, her gaze snagging on several familiar faces that sat around a long dark wooden table. Dr Jenkins, the workhouse's medical officer had a sober, glum disposition. He sat stiffly in his chair, his face grim and pale. Next to him, Mr Simmons, a slender, willowy man who had retired from his successful business and passed it to his sons, gave her a courteous nod.

"Good morning, everyone," Portia tried to sound confident though she heard the quiver in her voice.

She felt the attention as it crawled over her skin before she met the dark, inscrutable gaze of the man seated at the head of the table. *The Workhouse Master*. He'd been absent from her first meeting when she'd been interviewed, and her busy daily routine meant that she'd not yet met him.

During her interview, the guardians had explained to her then that he was a man consumed by grief, though Portia didn't see a scrap of sadness about him now. His face was an unreadable mask, his stare searing into her, provoking a tremor of unease. William Finnegan was indeed a handsome man, with neatly combed dark curls that were turning silver at the temples. His right hand rested on top of the papers stacked in front of him as he watched her. Lifting her chin, she met his stare head-on, her shoulders pushed back in a show of quiet defiance, even though her pulse pounded in her ears.

"Come, come," Mrs Draper flapped her hand in a half-wave, half-summons, indicating the vacant chair next to her.

Portia took the chair, noticing that William didn't bother standing for her in the same manner the other gentlemen did. She reminded herself that she was here to advocate for the children's education, and she would not be deterred by a room full of stern faces and harsh gazes.

"Thank you for agreeing to speak with me," she murmured as she took her seat, surreptitiously wiping her hands on the simple dark blue dress that she wore.

The parlour was painted white and the room was tastefully furnished. As with many of the rooms allocated to the staff, they were clean and well-kept. The fire was set but not lit, allowing for the warm sunny day that she could see through the wide window. Even from here, Portia could see just how much of the yards the location of the parlour allowed Mr Finnegan to see.

"Not at all," Mr Simmons responded, tucking himself back into his chair. "It's a good opportunity for you to meet some of the Board members. You already know the doctor and Mrs Draper. We have Mr Wright, who is our Clerk, Mr Davies is the Treasurer for the Board, and of course, you know Mr Finnegan."

"I've not yet had the opportunity," William's voice was stony, and when Portia met that shuttered gaze, she wanted to run away. "What with one thing and another, our paths have not yet crossed. My apologies for that oversight."

Portia forced her mouth into a smile. "Not at all, Mr Finnegan. You're a busy man. Being responsible for more than two hundred inmates is no mean feat."

He acknowledged the compliment with a slight

incline of his head. "Never a truer word, Miss Summerhill."

Mr Simmons leaned forward. "I'm quite curious to see how you've been getting on, Miss Summerhill."

"Unless you've requested to speak with us today to hand in your notice," Dr Jenkins added.

Mrs Draper seemed horrified by the idea, her eyes widening. "Is that what you're doing?"

"No, no," Portia's smile was genuine as she tried to ease the woman's worries. "I've only been here a fortnight."

"Long enough to resign from a job you despise," the man who'd been introduced as Mr Wright said.

"I'm not handing in my notice." She heard Mrs Draper's sigh of relief and wondered just how hard she'd fought to have the board hire a woman. "I am enjoying the post. The children are mostly well-behaved."

"Mostly?"

Portia offered a tentative smile to Mr Simmons and guessed him to be a second advocate for her. "My schoolroom is filled all day. I only have enough room to teach twenty or so at a time, yet there are over eighty children at the workhouse. I've tried to squeeze extra children in, but it can be difficult to have them all working. Unless they're occupied, they can become disruptive."

"You can't control them?"

Portia turned to William Finnegan. "I'm not saying that," she replied evenly.

Mr Simmons interjected, "Then what *are* you saying, Miss Summerhill?"

"I asked to speak to the Board because, as I understand it, you all oversee the operation and business of the workhouse, including its expenditure and budgets."

Several looks were exchanged before Mr Simmons warily confirmed this.

Portia continued. "The children have nothing to help them advance in their education. I'm seeking funds to replace books so that I can help them with their reading. Slates to learn and practice writing, perhaps an abacus–"

"Out of the question," Mr Finnegan snapped. "Funds are already limited, and we have a leak in the roof that will need attention before winter. That takes precedence before anything else."

"There are books in the schoolroom. We replaced many of them not that long ago," Mr Wright said. He had the appearance of a man who enjoyed the finer things in life and his expression matched the mocking tone, "You can teach them to read, can't you?"

"Four books between twenty-five children truly isn't a viable solution for teaching, Mr Wright."

Mr Wright's brows met, and he slid a glance at the workhouse master. "Only four? Out of all those books we purchased?"

"There are more than that," William stated impatiently. His look sharpened on his new schoolmistress, "That worthless Mr Park must have put them in a safe place. Have you searched the room properly?"

Portia nodded. "There are only four books, sir."

"Nonsense," William said, sitting up. She realised that he was uncomfortable with her pointing out faults in his establishment in front of the people he had to answer to and was getting ready to dismiss her.

"Perhaps you'd care to accompany me to the classroom, Mr Finnegan? I'd be more than happy to show you what tools the children have for their schooling."

His nostrils flared white with disapproval and his lips flattened in the stony silence that followed her comment. "Miss Summerhill –"

"Sorry, I'm late!" The door burst inwards and a rotund man with spectacles stumbled into the room, dabbing his balding head with a handker-chief. His twinkling eyes lit upon Portia, and he smiled. Reverend James was most definitely an advocate for her – she'd enjoyed a thoroughly entertaining conversation with him during her initial meeting. "Miss Summerhill – hello, my dear!"

"Oh, gosh," Mrs Draper muttered, her fluttering hands blocking off her nostrils just as the aroma of manure reached the group.

"There were cows out on the lane," the Reverend explained. "I helped John Clark funnel them back to where they should have been."

"Perhaps we ought to open a window," the doctor muttered, standing up to do just that. "Miss Summerhill was appealing to the board for funds to purchase equipment for the schoolroom."

Oblivious to the foul aroma that he'd brought in with him, Reverend James took a seat at the table, encouraging Portia with a nod. "Is that so? Well, I think that is a wonderful idea."

"Not everyone agrees with you, Reverend," Mrs Draper said shrilly.

The reverend frowned, his inquisitive gaze moving around the table. "Why ever not?"

"The roof," William told him, his tone considerably kinder than the one he'd been using only moments ago.

"What about it?" the Reverend asked.

"It needs repairing. How can we hope to keep everyone safe and dry if we have water cascading from upon high."

Portia's attention was drawn to the workhouse

master. Not only was his tone softer, but she could see affection seeping through his shuttered gaze.

The reverend pushed away his protest. "Billy, come on. You of all people ought to know the benefits of education," he turned to Portia, pride reflecting in his expression. "Billy was an inmate here, Miss Summerhill."

Portia's brows shot up, unable to keep the surprise from her face as she turned to look at William Finnegan. She could have sworn the strict Master was blushing. "I didn't know that."

"Yes," Reverend James confirmed. "Thanks to the intervention of several of the guardians – myself included at the time – he managed to better himself through education and knowledge. He worked his way through school, excelling in many areas. He studied chemistry at Cambridge.

One of my proudest moments was when he accepted the position here as Workhouse Master, to be able to give back to the Parish that helped him. One of the youngest men in the role, too!"

William shifted in his chair and shuffled the papers in front of him.

The reverend, oblivious to his embarrassment, continued, "Education elevates people, doesn't it? If we can raise the standard of education in our society, one might hope that the children will be less inclined to rely on the workhouse in the future.

If they can read and write, they will be better suited to many jobs, rather than seasonal labour or menial tasks. An enlightened person is a productive person, don't you agree, Miss Summerhill?"

Portia felt the flicker of hope roar to life as she nodded with enthusiasm. She opened her mouth to thank the reverend when she was interrupted.

"This is all very well in theory," Mr Davies spoke, his voice like a douse of cold water on her delight. "But we still have the matter of meeting the current needs for the workhouse. The roof, as Mr Finnegan has already mentioned, is just one item on the agenda.

We have the rat-catcher invoice to settle, though I must add that the amount seems extortionately high…"

"I submitted the quotes," William said briskly. "I have a receipt in my office."

"I thought we'd agreed that young Smout from the village would take on the job? His quote was the lowest, after all."

William looked gimlet-eyed at the Doctor who had spoken. "I went with the one from Madeley. He was able to do the job sooner than Smout."

"Mr Finnegan, I know that you've had a lot on your mind recently, but we do have a budget to keep to," Dr Jenkins linked his fingers together and rested his hands on the table in front of him. Portia could see the flare of disdain burning in his eyes when the two men looked at each other.

"Costs keep rising, Dr Jenkins. Costs that are quite beyond my control," William's voice was tight with anger.

The doctor quirked a brow, but it was Mr Davies who interrupted again. "The coal bill for last winter was much higher than previous years. We are surrounded by woods – can't you use some of that to fuel the fires?"

"If I had the staff to manage the inmates whilst out in the woods…" William said.

"They'll hardly abscond in their uniform," Mr Davies scoffed. "They stick out like a sore thumb whenever they go to church."

Portia's eyes darted around the table, wondering how to bring the subject of slates and books back into the discussion. She was quickly finding out just how running the workhouse was more than just charity work to some.

"I thought you'd agreed to use my man for the roof," Simmons interjected.

"I'm yet to see the invoice for the blankets purchased in the spring," Mr Wright pointed out.

William Finnegan's lips twitched, and his eyes narrowed on the clerk. "It's in my office. I shall fetch it before you leave."

"William is doing a bang-up job," Reverend

James declared. "We're all here to help, not to hinder. I know that you're not suggesting anything untoward with the missing receipts or misappropriation of funds, Mr Wright."

"Of course not," Mr. Wright admitted begrudgingly. "But the books have to balance."

"Gentleman, speaking of books?" Mrs Draper said, and Portia sent her a grateful look.

"If we could just –" Portia began but was cut off by an annoyed Mr Davies.

"Every meeting we have, William, you have admitted more lone children that have been abandoned at the gates. This is why overheads are spiralling. We are already beyond capacity."

"Is he supposed to turn the children away?" Mrs Draper's fingers trembled at her throat as she stared aghast around the table.

Mr Davies pressed all ten fingertips into the wooden surface to glare at her. "My point is that adult inmates earn back their keep through additional monies made selling the oakum strands to the navy or the stone chips to the road companies. They contribute skills through farming the livestock. Children are often inmates for longer, which only increases our food expenses."

"Some adults have been here for decades," Mrs Draper pointed out. "And I quite agree that we cannot turn children away."

"We don't have room for sentiment here," Mr Davies said. "This is all a delicate balance."

"I know," William's hard-edged voice was back, the expression deadpan. "I'm more than aware of what it takes to run this establishment, Mr Davies. It is the Board that offers indoor relief to these children. Perhaps if we could send some of them to one of the District Schools instead?"

"They're full," Mrs Draper said.

Round and round the discussion went. Arguments about missing receipts and invoices that were piling up. Portia tried to keep track though it was difficult with the undercurrents flowing around the room. William might harbour some tenderness toward the Reverend, but he didn't think much of the other guardians. It looked as if her pleas for equipment had fallen on deaf ears until the Reverend and Mrs Draper had teamed up against the rest of the board members.

As they decided on a generous budget for her, she felt that hard dark gaze from the other end of the table once more.

She may have won this battle but, as she left the room to return to her schoolroom, she was all too aware of just how annoyed William Finnegan was with his new schoolmistress.

CHAPTER 6

With the sound of the summer rain swishing against the windows, Maisie Milne sat in the women's day room. Her fingertips were marked by dark tar stains from the oakum, the skin split and tender from coarse rope strands. Despite the chill seeping up from the unforgiving stone floor, she persisted, the steady rhythm of the work a comforting monotony.

"I'm going to the kitchen to check the work in there," Matron Pursley announced to the room, her militant gaze surveying the bowed heads. The room was more cramped than usual because of the inclement weather. "If you want to eat tonight, you will get that basket emptied. I want one and a half pounds of rope picked from each person. Pick up the pace – *all* of you."

The door banged shut behind her. They waited until the key rattled in the door and the lock slid home before the whispered exchanges began.

"I can't work any faster, my fingers are stiff from the cold!"

"Can't we light the bleedin' fire?"

"Martha, you haven't done nearly as much as me – look!"

Maisie allowed the chatter to pass over her head. Usually, the aged and infirm took to the corner of the yard to do their work but today, all the women were crammed inside this one room. It was on days like this that scuffles amongst the inmates broke out. The bickering continued, growing in volume, as the women began to air their worries about all the recent changes at Brookford.

Their children, too young to be out in the world, were being taken away.

"I only see it as a good thing," Dilly Trent, her face marked with the lines of hard years and many seasons, waved off their concerns with a gruff hand. "I remember when it was just two to a bed. We're overrun now. Too many children are being left at the door. We can't keep taking them all in!"

"Why don't we hear where they end up though, Dilly?" Martha Cotton snapped. "Surely, they can't all be going into service jobs. And if they are? Servants are allowed regular days off. Wouldn't that child come back to see their family?"

"Would you come back here?" Dilly demanded, her voice low but firm. "Besides, you're forgetting the one constant with the children that don't come back – they're all orphans, by my count. Who are they going to come back and see?"

"That's rot, Dilly," Doris Gray, knitting by the back wall, shook her head with a snort.

She had come to the workhouse last winter for indoor relief when influenza took her husband. Childless and with no other means to support herself, she had resigned herself to life within these cold, confining walls. Doris was one of the lucky ones. She'd worked her whole life and was well-known in the parish. Her age and hard work had earned her some measure of leniency within the workhouse, and she had a seat rather than having to sit on the floor with the others. "One of the youngsters in the children's ward...I knew his mother. Mary Richards would never have abandoned that boy. Something terrible must have happened to her."

"Of course, it hasn't! Stop winding everyone up, Doris!"

Doris was unconvinced. "All I know is Mary Richards wanted a baby all her life. I haven't heard from anyone that the poor woman has snuffed it – have you?"

"Well, no," Dilly allowed.

"Then how did that poor boy find his way here if his mother is alive? I'm telling you, something's not adding up," Doris insisted, her eyes flashing with fierce determination.

Maisie listened; her attention diverted from her work. The sudden surge of children being sent out to work was alarming, it spoke of a desire to empty the workhouse of its younger occupants. Duncan was approaching the age where he could be apprenticed out to one of the local farms. His tall stature would mean that he would be snatched up by a brickmaker or an ironmonger. Maybe even sent to one of the cities for factory work. The prospect of losing her friend and then never hearing from him again filled her with dread.

Maisie recognised Maggie Sutton's voice cut through the fearful conjecture that rippled around the room. "Enough speculating! We're not in the world anymore; we're in here. We can't know what's happened out there."

Doris, unrelenting, continued her tirade. "There's too many changes...those books, for instance."

This time, Maisie looked up, defensiveness rising within. "What about the books?"

Doris peered down at her from the superior level. "We're sat in here, no fire lit because Matron says it's summertime and the workhouse can't afford the coal, but then, lo and behold, new books arrive! Books, I ask you! What do people like us need books and writing slates for?"

"I want to learn to write. Miss Summerhill tells us that we must learn to read and write so that we make society better." Contemptuous grunts rolled around the room, and Maisie frowned at them all. "What's wrong with wanting a better life than this?"

"Because you'll just end up back here, like we did," Martha snapped. "It's no good to hope, Maisie. You'll be apprenticed out and then just disappear like the rest, despite what that jumped up new schoolmistress says."

Maisie would admit that she'd had her doubts about the pretty Miss Summerhill when she'd first arrived. She'd been wary of her optimism and positivity – hadn't Mr Park started out the same? His enthusiasm had quickly waned over the long working hours. He'd grown impatient with the number of children he'd had stuffed into the schoolroom, and all too often, the noisiest in the room would be sent to the matron. Matron meant the cane.

Miss Summerhill spoke kindly to the children.

She had told them how she had learned to read and discovered a love for far-off places – some that she'd been lucky enough to visit. She'd informed them then that she was going to get them some equipment so that they could all learn to read and write.

To read a book, to write her name… that would be more than many of the women in here knew how to do. Most had only ever learned to read.

The old ways of learning meant that paupers did not need to learn to write. Maisie had been dubious of such grand promises from the schoolmistress, especially after listening to the sour comments from the others but then, just last week, boxes had arrived filled with dusty volumes filled with stories. Such strange titles like *Uncle Tom's Cabin* and *Alice in Wonderland*. Writing slates with slate pencils. An abacus with shiny wooden beads.

Maisie had listened to the rumours that she was the replacement for old Mrs Finnegan but with her chestnut hair, creamy skin, and sympathetic nature, she was the antithesis of the master's wife. There was a sincerity to her that was starting to thaw many of the workhouse children towards learning.

"I like her. She's nice," Maisie nodded.

"What about young Duncan?" Martha's eyes gleamed spitefully. "He'll be gone next!"

"You shut your mouth," Maisie snarled, tossing down the oakum.

"Leave the girl alone, Martha," Maggie Sutton intervened again. "She's already been in the broom cupboard this week. Maisie, ignore her."

"Maybe all these ups and downs are from old Mrs Finnegan. Her ghostly spirit lingering on to wreak havoc here where she died and make trouble for ol' Billy Finny!" Martha chuckled and was rewarded with a collective moan. Several people crossed themselves and whispered up a prayer.

"Martha! That's enough! You're borrowing trouble now," Maggie's voice was stern.

The soft sobbing from the corner drew the gazes of the inmates. Bessie Nichols covered her face with her filthy hands. "My David!"

Maisie sighed. Bessie's son was one of the boys who'd vanished. She hadn't heard from the boy since the day she'd been told he'd started an apprenticeship. She didn't know where or what her son was doing. She hadn't even been able to say goodbye to him. Maisie knew enough about him to know that David wouldn't have left his mother's side without a fight.

Something wasn't adding up.

Maisie watched as Bessie was comforted by the other women nearby. She listened to the plaintive wailing and the assurances that Doris and Martha were just being their usual mean selves, but fretfulness niggled at Maisie.

Doris was right about one thing – too many changes were never good, in her book. Her life had been routine ever since she'd arrived at Brookford. Day after day, with people entering or dying. Those who left inevitably returned. Then Mrs Finnegan was found dead and suddenly everything changed.

Maisie shuddered. The talk of ghosts and spirits had upset everyone, and she knew that she wouldn't be getting much sleep tonight.

CHAPTER 7

"What is a foundling?"

The top blue fabric of the book was worn, and the board was poking out at the edges. Maisie ran her fingers over the title embossed into the cover. It had taken her a while to decipher the word.

"A foundling is a baby that has been abandoned and then cared for by others."

"Like an orphan?" Maisie asked.

Miss Summerhill smiled and shook her head slightly. "Not exactly. An orphan is a child whose parents have died. A foundling's parents may still be alive, but they have had to give up the child for various reasons."

Maisie had volunteered to stay behind and help

Miss Summerhill tidy up the schoolroom once the afternoon lessons had finished. The schoolroom was small, considering the number of children at the workhouse. With its whitewashed walls and high narrow windows at the far end that allowed a little of the daylight through, the space had been utilised economically. Rows of hard wooden benches were arranged with regimented precision, designed more for order and discipline than comfort or ease of use. The desks were well-worn, covered with notches and scratches from countless hands over the years.

The new room additions, other than the books that now filled the bookcases, included a world map that was curled at the edges. Miss Summerhill had explained that the map used to belong to one of the guardians, as well as most of the books that they'd had donated. A world globe, faded and scratched, rested on a pedestal near the chalkboard, a silent symbol of the world beyond the workhouse walls.

To Maisie, the room had always smelled musty, with its chalk dust and damp walls. She couldn't recall the last time the small stove in the corner of the room had been lit.

Maisie had wiped down the slate boards, removing the scratchings of the other children, where they had copied Miss Summerhill's letters from the blackboard set on the easel at the front of the room. She had straightened the benches and set the slate pencils at the side of each grey board.

She enjoyed listening to Miss Summerhill's lessons. The teacher didn't mock or shout, nor was she yet to use her cane on some of the naughtier children.

Maisie slotted the book into the bookcase, having to use both hands to do so. "I'm an orphan, not a foundling. My mother died the night I arrived here."

Something sad moved behind the teacher's eyes as she stared at Maisie. Maisie wanted to fidget under the strange look that she was giving her. "I'm so very sorry, Maisie. What did she die of?"

"Couldn't tell you. I don't remember anything about her."

"Not a thing?"

The gentle way in which she asked the question made Maisie's eyes sting a little. She blinked, knowing that tears never helped. "No, Miss."

"How old were you when you got here?"

"Four."

"That's awfully young, Maisie," Portia said kindly. Maisie nibbled at her lower lip, knowing the pain of biting into the soft flesh would stem the flow of tears. "Memory can be distorted through the years."

"I was four," Maisie said again with a firm nod.

"How do you know? You might have been younger!"

"Old Franny Harp told me," Maisie replied, expanding on her answer when Miss Summerhill asked. "She died the winter before last. She'd lived at the workhouse for years. She found me crying for my mama the day after I'd arrived. I'd told her how old I was then. She might have been mad as a box of frogs in the end, but she could recall random things like that.

She was the only one who believed that my mother was with me. Everyone else thinks I was abandoned here but… I remember…"

Just like that, the memory she'd been reaching for exploded behind her mind's eye. Her mother, bedraggled, clutching a baby. John Cobb smiling at her pretty mother. How the pie slice glistened in the soft light from the wall sconces in the porter's room as the plate was set down in front of them. *Just like Nellie Jones had said.*

Her breath left her body in a whoosh and her gaze collided with the teacher.

"I remember," she whispered, unable to stop the tears this time.

"What do you remember, Maisie?"

Maisie risked a look at the teacher. Instead of scepticism, she saw only trust. "Everything, now. But back then? Not so much. I was so confused, but I can see Franny Harp now as clearly as if she was still sitting here next to you.

I was crying for Ma. The other children told me that I was wrong. It was Franny who scooped me up and rocked me, so I'd stop my bellyaching. She told me that it was Mr Finnegan's job as work-house master to write down the births and deaths of the people who entered the workhouse. She told me to go and ask for myself.

I asked Mrs Finnegan to check what my Ma had died of. I wanted to know whether she'd been buried in this parish or not. I don't remember going to the funeral. Not that they'd ring the bell for a pauper, mind."

"What do you mean?"

"The parish church bell toll for each year of life at a funeral, doesn't it? When someone dies. If they die at thirty, it rings thirty times. Well, not when you die a pauper. My mother might only have a simple cross to mark where she ended up, but she also deserves someone to weep for her."

"What did it show your Mama died of?"

Maisie swallowed and her eyes grew hot. "At first, Matron Finnegan refused to tell me. She locked me in the broom cupboard when I pressed her on it. Still, I needed to know."

"And?"

"She said that I was abandoned at the gates like the rest of the unfortunates."

"Are you certain you arrived with someone? We remember things differently as we get older."

Maisie rounded on the schoolmistress, temper sparks flying as hurt ripped through her. She banged her fist on the desk. "You don't believe me either?"

Miss Summerhill lifted her hands, quickly trying to reassure her. "That's not what I meant, Maisie. Maybe your mother dropped you off here. Maybe she had no choice but to–"

"I remember someone being in that waiting room with me!" Maisie stated through gritted teeth. "I remember there being a baby born. I know that baby was with us. I *remember* it, Miss Summerhill." Shimmering images floated through her mind. Sometimes, she'd wondered if it was a dream – a vivid dream of another lifetime. Yet now she knew was certain. *A sibling.*

What had happened to them both?

Frustration at not knowing everything formed a hot ball in her belly. She fought her tears, making fists at her sides. Miss Summerhill had been kind to her. Could she be trusted with the scant memories she had of that night?

"When Mrs Finnegan told me I'd been left out by the gates, I called her a liar to her face. She beat me a good 'un for my cheek, chopped off my hair so that everyone would know I was a troublemaker." She heard the soft gasp of horror emitted by the teacher and pressed on, her voice thickening with unshed tears. "You might not believe me, but I know I wasn't at the gates. I remember walking up the path. I remember standing in the Porter's room. I remember John Cobb," she added with a fierce whisper.

Portia crouched down so that she was at Maisie's eye level. "I'm sorry if you think I doubted you. I believe you, Maisie."

Maisie swallowed as the teacher blurred through her tears. "You do?"

"Yes." The answer was simple in its truth, but the word meant more to Maisie than anything she'd heard before. "I believe you."

The fight went out of her rigid body, and she exhaled. She nodded, knuckling away the tears that slipped down her cheeks. "Thank you."

"You've been here at Brookford many years, Maisie. Learning the way that you do will go a long way to building a life where you never have to rely on the workhouse system when you get older." The words felt complimentary, and Maisie smiled a little. Miss Summerhill asked, "Can you tell me how many years you've lived here?"

Maisie lifted a bony shoulder. "Well, I was four when I arrived. I'll be fourteen on my next birthday."

"And so how many years is that?"

Maisie screwed up her face as she tried to think. Recalling what Miss Summerhill had taught her, she rearranged the numbers in her mind. "Ten!"

Miss Summerhill's smile was broad. "You're a very fast learner, Maisie. You'll soon be reading *The History of Tom Jones* by yourself."

"I like reading."

"So do I. I like having a world created around me and escaping into it."

Maisie stopped fiddling with the slate pencils to stare at the teacher. She'd been here for two months almost and yet, in such a short space of time, she'd managed to make several changes already. She couldn't help but wonder what made a woman like Miss Summerhill choose to work here, of all places. "What's your favourite book?"

Miss Summerhill smiled and straightened up. She lifted the lid of her desk and held up a dog-eared book. "This." She set the book down and Maisie waited until she'd been permitted to pick it up before she touched up.

"P-P... Prom..etheus? What kind of word is *Prometheus?*"

"It's from Greek mythology. Prometheus was a demi-god who stole fire from Olympus and gave it to men so that they had it here on Earth when it was only meant to be for the gods. It means 'fore thinker'. Prometheus was a trickster."

"This book is about a trickster?" Maisie tilted it, her nose wrinkling. "I think I'd like to know more."

Miss Summerhill chuckled softly. "This book is quite dark, Maisie. It's about a scientist who dabbled in things he shouldn't and created a man from..." She stopped and raised her eyes from the worn book cover to look at Maisie. Her lips curved upwards. "Yes, a little too dark for a young mind like yours. Saying that, Mary Shelley was only eighteen when she started writing it."

Maisie's mouth dropped open. "A woman wrote it?"

"She did, yes. Just like the Brontë sisters, she had to write it anonymously."

Maisie practised the new word quietly, rolling it around in her mouth.

Miss Summerhill watched the action, smiling. "It means to do something where you cannot be identified by name. You should try using it in a sentence for me."

Maise pondered a moment. "Maisie Milne was left at the workhouse anonymously."

Miss Summerhill laughed then and cupped her cheek, drawing a smile out of Maisie, too. "I was right – you're too bright for your own good. What do you want to do when you leave here? Have you thought much about it?"

Maisie set the book down on Miss Summerhill's desk. "No point."

The schoolmistress paused. "There's every point, Maisie. You have your whole life ahead of you."

"Easy for you to say. You're clever. You have a proper job, though why you'd choose to work here instead of a real school, I don't know."

"Because I came from a poor start, just like you."

Maisie's nose crinkled again, tilting her head. "You came from a workhouse?"

Miss Summerhill cleared her throat and then turned her back to Maisie. She began to line up the pieces of chalk along the divot in the frame of the easel. "Um, no. Not quite. My aunt... she rescued me. She educated me, took me travelling with her."

"I should like to travel. Go to Liverpool and see the boats that they stuff full of the oakum we split." It was hard to imagine what life would be like once she was able to leave here. For so many years, it had seemed like a distant dream. "Once I'm fourteen, I can be chosen by an employer. Maybe a servant. A ladies' maid," she murmured, toying with the fanciful idea of living in a grand house. She gave her head a little shake to cast out such farfetched thinking. "Not that I want to be apprenticed out."

"Why ever not?"

"Haven't you heard the talk? People disappear from here all the time."

Miss Summerhill's hand stilled, and she slowly pivoted to stare at her. Her mouth snapped shut and she moved her lips. "W-what talk?"

Maisie lifted a shoulder nonchalantly, thinking about the conversation in the day room in the summer, and countless more since. "I'm not the only child who says that their mother or father brought them in. And the children that have been given jobs recently? None of them have been seen since."

"The children that have been apprenticed out might have been sent out of county," the teacher said carefully, dusting off her hands. "Apprentices don't earn a great deal. Most of their wages will probably have to go on food and lodgings. And unfortunately, people die, Maisie. All the time. It's a sad fact of life that I'm sure you don't need explaining when you've grown up in a place such as this."

"That's right, they do," Maisie said matter-offactly. "But dead people tend to get buried, don't they? And I don't remember the last time anyone from here went to a funeral."

A bell rang deep in the belly of the building, signalling the end of the workday. Maisie smiled at the teacher. "Thank you for today's lesson, Miss Summerhill." She skipped to the door and let herself out, not seeing the shock still rippling across the face of the schoolmistress.

CHAPTER 8

*P*ortia walked towards Matron's office, a sense of apprehension making each step feel heavier than the last. Even though in her role, she had daily interactions with the other woman, it did not mean that she enjoyed them. She found her somewhat callous. Just that afternoon when she'd been escorting her cohort of children out into the yard for their outdoor exercise, she'd witnessed a heated quarrel between Matron and a mother who was trying to stop Mrs Pursley from moving her child up into the older group and away from her. Portia had smoothly intervened and taken the sobbing woman inside to comfort her.

Still, she had a job to do, and so, with a deep breath, she knocked on the scuffed wooden door.

"Enter," came the clipped voice from within.

The door creaked as she opened it. Matron Pursley was sitting behind her cluttered desk, an annoyed expression etched into her features as the candlelight flickered over her face, casting strange, dancing shadows on the walls.

The fire roared in the hearth, providing a sharp contrast to the chill of the workhouse. The room was a cavern of heavy drapes and shadows, populated by trinkets and curios scattered across the furniture that added grandeur, souvenirs of a life lived outside the workhouse. Portia tried not to stare as she stepped inside. The sitting room was almost the same size as her schoolroom, and she could see the bed-chamber through the open door behind Mrs Pursley.

"Matron, do you have a minute?" Portia asked, her voice steady despite her unease. "I wanted to ask you something."

Matron Pursley glanced over at her; one thick eyebrow raised in question. With a begrudging sigh, she gestured towards the vacant chair opposite her.

"I suppose I do," she said. "Sit. Would you like some tea?" She gestured towards a gilded teapot and a half-empty bowl of sugar cubes on the side table. Crumbs remained on a dish, remnants of a sweet biscuit or some such treat, no doubt. Portia had to swallow down the swell of annoyance at the sight, thinking of the times Matron had withheld food from the inmates as a form of punishment.

"No, thank you," Portia declined politely as she took a seat. She waited until Matron had sweetened her drink and sat back down, the chair groaning in protest as she did.

Matron drew the cup closer to her and she gave Portia a sharp-eyed look. "I'm glad you are here, where we might speak in private. I have something to say to you, also."

Portia bit back a sigh and invited the woman to speak first.

"As I understand it, this job is your first foray into employment and so I have let a lot of your... sympathies slide," Mrs Pursley pushed some papers pointlessly to one side, her expression peevish as she glared across her desk. Portia could see all too well just how much her interruption of the quarrel in the yard earlier had irked her. "The systems and routines that we have in place have been that way for decades, Miss Summerhill. You cannot allow your finer feelings at just how hard life must seem here to someone delicate like yourself to cloud your judgement. I've warned you over and over that these people will spot a weak link in the chain, and they will break it."

"My finer feelings?"

"Yes," Matron snapped. "You're too soft. Fragile.

Inmates need to be ruled, or else they will revolt. We have rules so that we might maintain order. You are a woman. We are weaker, softer. It would take nothing for one of those wretches to coldcock you and then dine on your bones. I've seen how you are with the imbeciles, Miss Summerhill. You must keep your distance, or else you will lose control.

I've spoken with Mr Finnegan and Mr Cobb, and they agree with me. As Matron here at Brookford, it falls within my remit to guide you. You are to stop this feebleness at once. And never question my direction ever again."

Portia folded her arms as she stared across the desk. "I see. So, I am to use force with a woman older than my dear aunt? Berate a person simply because they cannot comprehend complex language? Or rip a child from a sobbing mother, instead of using a little compassion to comfort that woman?"

The matron leaned forward, setting her elbow on the table, and stabbing her index finger into the surface to make her point. "If this insubordination continues, I shall have no choice but to recommend that the master seek an alternative schoolmistress. Perhaps someone more suited to the role."

The spike of irritation ran through Portia. She knew that her job was set by the guardians, not this woman and that she could appeal any such recommendations made by the master in front of the Board. But she was also aware that her position here was tenuous at best. The Board had taken a gamble by hiring a woman.

Portia fostered that flame of anger that burned within, a sign that she still had her humanity. She wanted to tell this curmudgeon that she would happily sing from the rooftops about the levels of unnecessary force happening within these walls that went against the rules set out by the laws of this land. She met the woman's glare from across the table as she weighed the choices laid before her. Would she be able to find another job after causing problems here? She might need a character reference in the future. After all, she understood more than most how fortunes could change in the blink of an eye. For now, she needed to be here.

Still, she wasn't prepared to start wielding the birch cane because Matron told her so. "I admit that I shouldn't have undermined you in front of the other women, Matron. My decision was poorly timed, and I can see now that I should have spoken to you in private about the issue," Portia caught the flare of triumph in Mrs Pursley's eyes before she continued, "but I can assure you that I am well aware of how hard life can be. It is our duty to provide guidance to these people, to show them how to behave in society."

"If you make it too pleasant here, then they won't want to leave."

"Some of them cannot leave, Matron," Portia said firmly. "Things happen beyond their control. Surely it is up to us to teach them how proper ladies act whilst they're here so that if and when they are able to return to the world beyond these walls, they are able to build a better life for themselves and can do so with decorum that they have learned from you and I."

Matron's eyes narrowed. Her lips formed a tight ring of displeasure. "We shall have to agree to disagree on that subject. I shall let the master know that we have spoken and that you have apologised."

She hadn't done any such thing, but Portia chose to let it slide.

"Now, what did you want to speak to me about?"

"I wanted to ask about the...procedure for funerals for the inmates here."

Matron's eyebrows furrowed in confusion, and she paused mid-sip of her tea. "Why on earth would you need to know about that?"

"As you said yourself, I've only been here two months. I'm just...still getting to grips with the way things are done here," Portia explained hastily.

"There are so many rules and regulations to know about. For example, one of the children asked about a funeral, and I wasn't sure what the process was.

I told the child that I would check that detail and, with your deep understanding about the job role, I knew that you were the right person to come to." Portia could see the compliment had hit the spot as the matron preened a little. "I just want to understand."

Matron eyed Portia over the rim of the cup for a few minutes. Portia had to wait patiently as she took several sips of the steaming liquid and Portia wondered if the other woman was debating how much to tell her, or if she was just being deliberately obstructive to get her back for today's fiasco.

Matron sighed and set her cup down. "When an inmate passes away, the death is recorded by Mr Finnegan. The Medical Officer will record the cause of death if known. Mr Finnegan will need to know where the home parish is, and this will have been recorded upon admission.

It's not our responsibility to bear the costs of having to bury a body. Poor Mr Finnegan must strike a fine balance to keep us all in work and these unfortunates housed. The body stays in the dead house until someone can collect the body to return it to whence it came. Local inmates are buried as a pauper in the local graveyard."

"So, a person might not be buried locally, then?" Portia clarified.

"No, not if the body is claimed by surviving family or friends," Matron toyed with the dainty cup. "Death is as much of a part of life, Miss Summerhill. You should not get too attached to the people here. Sentimentality has no part in a place like this. When an inmate dies, there will always be ten more seeking relief at our front doors not too long after. So, when one of them dies, I see it as one less mouth to feed. We are already bulging at the seams here," she added and leaned back in her chair, her face briefly softening. "Brookford is struggling under the weight of those it must care for. Mr Finnegan is petitioning the guardians for funds to build an extension to the building, but it's an uphill battle.

He is a shining example of how well a man can do when he applies himself. You're aware that Mr Finnegan was an inmate here himself, once upon a time."

Portia moved her mouth into a smile and nodded, just as she was meant to.

A soft light moved through Matron's eyes, and Portia shifted, uncomfortable at the fond affection that the other woman clearly held for him. The possibility of a romantic involvement between the two was an unsettling thought. Maybe it was because their jobs were so closely intertwined.

"He came back here with the idea to make this place better than when he was here. The old workhouse master was a cruel and evil man. Rumours have always clouded this place locally, but Mr Finnegan is a devout Christian who has the courage of conviction in his path to make Brookford a shining example for other workhouses to follow."

Portia kept any opinions on the capability and aptitude of a man to drag himself out of here when he had undoubtedly been helped and supported by the delightful Reverend James. She thought of all the children – those bright and inquisitive minds – who slumped over their desks in her schoolroom, desperately hungry and beaten. She had to wonder how well they could all do if they had a wealthy benefactor instead of a matron who wielded the cane with brute force.

"That's a brave ethos to have in these challenging times," Portia murmured.

"It was one that must have been shared by both the master and his late wife. Such a big responsibility for his young shoulders."

"Did you know Mrs Finnegan personally?"

"I never had the privilege, but she is spoken

with much fondness by those who knew her," Matron replied, picking up her cup once more.

Portia knew how the late Mrs Finnegan was spoken about by those who had languished under her care. The main emotion around her sudden death appeared to be one of relief, rather than sadness.

"It must be a change for everyone under their care. To have a married couple and now, several new staff instead."

"Well," Matron's cheek pinked a little, her attention back on shuffling the papers on her desk. "They were married, of course, but they didn't have children. There are married couples who both live and work together in other workhouses. With some degree of success, but I know that the master didn't share a bed chamber with his late wife. Some of her belongings were in my room when I first arrived here, so they slept separately, as all well-behaved married couples should.

Mr Wright let slip that they weren't a harmonious pair. Perhaps it was the age gap. You can tell Master Finnegan has such vitality for life."

Portia's brows climbed her head, but she kept quiet.

"Poor Mr Finnegan," Matron said again, shaking her head. "I dare say he wouldn't like to hear me say such things. He is a proud man, stoic and strong. To continue in his role here whilst he is grieving speaks to his dedication to his cause."

"It was the back staircase, wasn't it?"

Matron nodded absently, her mind elsewhere. "What she was doing on that side of the house at night is beyond me. I'm always careful on staircases but why was she in the men's wing at night..." Her eyes lifted from their contemplation of the patterns painted on her china cup, suddenly aware that she was saying more than she wanted to.

Her eyes flashed and she fixed Portia with a cold stare. "This brings me back to my earlier point: You don't allow yourself to grow sentimental with any of these heathens. You turn your back to them for a second, and you could find yourself at the foot of the staircase with a broken neck."

Portia's lips parted with shock. "Are you saying that you think someone here pushed–"

"If that will be all, Miss Summerhill, I still have work to do before I turn in for the night," Mrs Pursley cut her off mid-sentence. Without waiting, she stood and walked to the door. Portia felt the chilly air that seeped through the open door as she braced her hands on the wooden arms of her chair and stood up, her mind reeling.

Instead of answering her questions, a whole host of others now clamoured for attention. All these weeks, she'd assumed that Mrs Finnegan had simply walked out of her room, lost her balance, and tumbled down the stairs in the dead of night. It seemed the most feasible answer. Portia couldn't walk up the same staircase to her room without shuddering at the thought. She reached the doorway and paused, needing to know more but Mrs Pursley swept a hand through the air.

"Good night, Miss Summerhill," she said pointedly.

Portia had no choice but to step through, leaving Matron to her warmth and her sugar cubes. "Good night, Mrs Pursley. Thank you for your help."

She crossed the short landing between their doors and let herself into her room, leaning back against the cool surface, her mind racing.

What had Mrs Finnegan been doing on the wrong side of the house at night?

CHAPTER 9

"I don't like her," Maud Whitby muttered.

Maisie stared at the girl. "Why ever not?"

"I don't trust her. She says we have to sit in that room and learn to help us. My Da learned to read and write. He still ended up down the mills, dead before my brother was born. Coughed his'self to death," Maud nodded to the captive audience. "What is the likes of us going to do with books?"

A grumbling of assent rolled around the small group of children who were standing in the yard. September rain had washed the sky blue. Deep puddles had formed along the outer wall, pooling in the corners. There was a snap of autumn in the air. David Jones raced past with his stick and hoop, hooting like a train. Maisie was keeping an eye on the door of the workhouse, waiting for Duncan, when Maud's loud voice caught her attention whilst slating Miss Summerhill. Naturally, Maisie had gone to the school mistress's rescue.

"Don't you see that that is precisely why we need books? Your father, God rest his soul, was a man. I'm sorry about his death, but his death wasn't caused because he'd learned to read. It was probably consumption. Heck, he was local so was probably down the mines as a boy." Maud's expression glowered. Maisie pressed on before the foghorn that was Maud Whitby sounded again. "If we are to stand any chance for ourselves, for any children we may have, we need a fighting chance."

Maud scoffed and waved a hand in front of her face. "Poppycock! You are just Summerhill's bootlicker!"

"Toady Maisie," another sniggered.

Maisie tried not to let the names get under her skin. "You shut your cake hole, Maud Whitby!"

A grin twisted Maud's mouth and triumph lit up her eyes. "Make me."

Anger flashed through her body. Mid-leap, an arm snaked around her waist and dragged her back. Maisie struggled until she realised that it was Duncan's arm.

"She's not worth it," his voice rumbled in her

ear, and she allowed him to pull her away from the group of jeering children.

Impotent tears stung her eyes as she glared around him. "I hate them. Spiteful and ungrateful miscreants."

"Miscreants?" Amusement laced through Duncan's voice which only kicked at her temper more.

She angled her chin upwards and was about to tell him how Miss Summerhill had taught her such a word when she saw his face. The words died on her lips, and she instinctively reached out to touch the bruise that marred the left side of his face. "What happened to you?"

Duncan lifted a hand to still the action and ducked out of the way. "Nothing."

"It doesn't look like nothing. Who did this?"

Duncan's eyes darted about. "Lower your voice, Maisie. Don't make trouble."

Maisie's eyes stung from helpless anger, and she blinked away the hot tears that burned her eyes. "I hate it here, Duncan. From one moment to the next, I hate it. We get beaten by the staff and now we're turning on each other?"

"It wasn't an inmate," he murmured, patting the air to try and calm her down. It wasn't until she felt the pressure of his touch on her shoulders that the shaking began to ease. "John Cobb told me I wasn't working fast enough, even though I'd done more work than most of the others. You know how he can get sometimes."

Fury, hot and searing, spilt over as her eyes sought out Nellie Jones. The pretty newcomer was dancing in a circle as she held hands with some of the children, singing Ring-o-Roses. Maisie grabbed at Duncan's wrist and made to pull him toward the other woman, to show her exactly what her porter 'friend' had done, but Duncan was immovable.

"I want to show Nellie Jones exactly what her beloved John Cobb has done to you," Maisie told him, looking up at his battered face.

Duncan shook his head. "And what would be the point? Cobb would deny it and Nellie would never believe you. Everyone knows she has a soft spot for him. Let sleeping dogs lie.

As soon as I can, I'll be out of here. I'll find some work. I have a plan; you wait and see. I'm going to speak to the landowner that my parents worked for. My father had a good reputation in the area, surely that would work in my favour?"

A wan smile touched Maisie's mouth. "Any landowner would be lucky to have you, Duncan."

"Why are you crying?" Duncan asked, reaching up to swipe away a tear rolling down her cheek.

"Because hearing you talk about leaving makes me sad," Maisie admitted. "Things feel different now. Maybe it's because we are both older and change is imminent. I want nothing but good for you, Duncan. It's what you deserve, but the thought of never seeing you again is almost unbearable."

The light danced in Duncan's bright blue eyes as he gently cradled her face, his touch tender despite the roughness of his palms. "Maisie, you're my only friend. No matter where I end up, do you think I'd leave you in a place like this any longer than necessary?"

A line formed between Maisie's brows. "What do you mean?"

Duncan took a moment as though trying to formulate his words, running the tip of his tongue along his top teeth. "Don't you know? Maisie, you're the last thought I have before I close my eyes and the first thing on my mind when I wake. Even when I was sleeping in my own bed back home in the cottage, I would wonder about you... about how you were. As bleak as this place is, and regardless of how my parents felt about returning here each winter, I looked forward to it, knowing I'd see my only friend."

With Duncan there to dry her tears, the noises from the yard faded away, and only the warmth of his gaze remained. She had often wondered if Duncan's feelings mirrored her own.

A lopsided grin appeared on Duncan's face. "I

dream of a life where you're always a part of it, Maisie. I have hopes of finding a job on a farm, saving up enough to buy you a mangle so you can do the laundry, and then while you earn from that, I'd work the land. My mother always said I was being fanciful thinking of such things, mind."

Emotion squeezed her. He'd spoken of sharing a life with her to others, to those who were important to him. That meant more to her than anything else. "It's not a fanciful thought," Maisie whispered, her mind filled with dreams of a life alongside Duncan. "But who knows where we'll end up when we're apprenticed out? I don't want to be one of the ones who disappear, as so many seem to do."

Duncan firmly said, "I'd find you, no matter where you are. Any city or town in this country. Beyond the borders of this country, if needed. I would walk barefoot until my feet were raw if it meant finding you again, Maisie Milne."

As the sun sunk lower, casting long shadows across the workhouse yard, Maisie dared to dream. She dared to believe in Duncan, in their future, in the possibility that lay beyond these walls. Of a life outside the workhouse, of a life where bruises didn't mark their days, and fear didn't haunt their nights.

"We wouldn't be in here because someone else

decided it. We would have a say in our life, Maisie. And that makes all the difference.

"What do you say?" He asked, his voice dropping to a conspiratorial whisper. "Would a simple life with someone like me suit you?"

She searched his face. His beautiful yet battered face smiled down at her. Trust unfurled in her heart. A feeling that, in a place such as this, was more precious to her than gold. With her hand in his, the promise of a better life felt within reach. And it was enough. For now.

CHAPTER 10

*A*lthough the day had started out fine, by the time Portia was heading back along the narrow lane towards Brookford, the sky had turned ominously full of dark rain clouds.

She berated herself for the seemingly frivolous decisions she had made that day. Had she caught the earlier omnibus back, she would have been safely ensconced in her room by now. Still, today was the first time she'd been allowed any time off since she'd started her job and she'd had several errands to do.

The pretty town had been a welcome change from seeing pale faces all around her etched with such sadness. The clatter of hooves on cobbled stones and the laughter and warm babble of the people out on the streets were almost too much for her senses.

She hefted the basket further along her arm and glancing upwards, she lengthened her stride a little more to try and outrun the threatening downpour. Wind gusts rustled through the trees, causing the leaves to tumble and eddy through the air. Perhaps she'd been a little reluctant to return to Brookford, too. It was like a world of its own, tucked away and ruled by an iron fist that allowed very little sunlight in.

The little town had everything that she needed to complete her list of tasks that day. The cobbler had mended her boots, and she'd posted two letters. She'd enjoyed lunch in the park and had watched the swans gliding along the River Severn as she ate. The leisurely stroll along the road and browsing in shop windows to admire items that she knew she couldn't buy had been a pleasant distraction. Those small, simple luxuries of the outside world were in stark contrast to the bleak life within the workhouse's walls. For a few hours, she'd forgotten about austerity and monotony. Yet, as she now rushed back, guilt pricked her conscience; the ones she cared for in the workhouse didn't have the luxury to escape, even for a moment.

The whispering wind was interrupted by what

sounded like an infant's cry. Portia slowed, wondering if she was hearing things. But there it was again, clear as day, just as the first splatters of rain began to fall. She stopped, straining her ears, trying to pinpoint the noise.

She approached the hedgerow and spotted a stile tucked within the brambles. She peered into the thicket of trees, peering through the gloom. She caught the quiet female murmuring, trying to soothe the lamenting baby.

With caution, Portia climbed over the stile, her basket swinging as she balanced herself. On the other side, the ground was soft and mossy, muffling her footsteps. A few steps in, she spotted a woman huddled beneath a tree, her back to Portia. The bundle that she clutched close to her chest wailed again.

"Hello?" Portia ventured.

The woman jumped, her head snapping around. The baby's cries grew louder, more distressed. Trying to soothe the infant, the woman looked Portia up and down, eyes wide with fright.

Portia took in her appearance: she was painfully thin, with a sallow complexion that spoke of illness or malnutrition. But her clothes, albeit modest, gave the impression that she was not always in this state. The rain, now steady, plunked on the leaves overhead, each droplet creating a rhythmic sound.

"I'm sorry," Portia said, taking a tentative step closer, "I didn't mean to frighten you."

The woman's eyes darted around her. "What do you want?" she demanded.

"I heard your child," Portia replied gently, indicating the woods around them. "What are you doing out here?"

"What's it to you?" the woman snapped.

Portia offered a gentle smile, hoping to calm the young mother. "I don't mean any harm. My name is Portia Summerhill. What's yours?"

The woman hesitated, her fingers playing with the ragged cloth around her child. "Mrs Elsie Evans," she muttered, her eyes on her baby. "This is Thomas."

"It's nice to meet you," Portia said, treading lightly. "Are you on your way somewhere?"

Elsie nodded, her chin set. "I thought I'd get out of this rain. Thomas here… he's probably hungry but…" she gestured helplessly at her chest. "Nothing is coming out."

A rush of pity stormed through her. The child was starving because his mother was, too. "Where are you headed?"

Elsie dragged a hand down her face, looking up through the canopy of trees. Fat drops of rain splattered her face, and she held her mouth open, her tongue out.

Portia tried again. "Where is your husband?"

The response was cold and filled with pain. "Dead."

The weight of that single word hung in the air, as the rain continued its relentless descent. Portia felt awkward, and out of place, yet felt compelled to stay and help the woman.

Thomas squirmed again. Elsie fiddled with the filthy wrappings, the faint wails settling as she rocked him gently. "Died last month," she said softly. "Just upped and left me. Me and the bairn… we're alone."

"I'm sorry," Portia murmured.

"What for?" Elsie's voice lashed at her. "You didn't kill him, did yer?"

"Well, no," Portia tried to amend. "It's just what one says…"

"Never did understand that saying. You didn't know him. You don't know me."

Portia's indignation softened when she caught the shine of tears when Elsie looked up at her. "You're right, of course. I didn't know him, nor do I know you. But I'd like to help you if I can. Because you can't stay out here. Thomas is too young to be out in a rainstorm. And you look as if you'll be swept away in the winds, too."

Elsie rubbed her lips across Thomas's downy head. "I was on my way to the workhouse, for indoor relief. My husband wouldn't like that I've come to this but... well, he isn't here, is he?" Her voice hardened, although she was mostly talking to herself. "We had a little room above the blacksmiths. With my Charlie gone, I... I can't meet the rent. I tried taking in washing and mending a few things but... well, food is expensive, isn't it, Miss?"

"Yes, I suppose it is when there's only one of you earning."

"Thomas here, he's all I have left of Charlie."

Portia's heart bruised a little when she heard the dull acceptance in the other woman's voice. "I work at Brookford. I'm the schoolmistress there."

"Schoolmistress?" Elsie's eyes focused on her. Portia could see her waxy pallor and wondered if perhaps what had killed Charlie also ailed her. "Never went to school. My father said there was no point."

A faint smile touched Portia's mouth. "If I had a ha'penny every time I heard that, Elsie, I'd be a wealthy woman."

Elsie slumped back with a sigh, swiping a hand over her damp head. "I had to sit down for a while, lest I fall down. I can't sit here all day, but it might be the last time I ever breathe in fresh air."

"Would you like me to walk with you? I'm heading back that way as it is."

Elsie looked at her for a moment, then rested her head against the tree. "I'm not sure as I can."

"Well, why don't I sit with you whilst you rest?"

"You don't have to, Miss."

"I know," Portia nudged a log to make sure that there were no hidden beasties on it before she lowered herself down. "How old is your son?"

"He was born in May," she said, a wistful smile brushing across her lips as she stroked his cheek. "How old does that make him?"

"Just over three months – give or take."

Elsie harumphed. "Maybe if I had gone to school, I'd not be in this situation right now."

"If your situation had been different, would you have met Charlie?"

The smile that bloomed on her face was touched with grief. "That's true enough," she said. "He was a good and kind man, doted on his boy. Proud as punch that he'd sired a son, too."

"Where did you meet him?"

"At the fair, miss. Father had a stall and we travelled with the fair, going from town to town, trying to sell his potions and the like."

Portia's brows climbed her forehead. "You're not local?"

Elsie shook her head. "Staffordshire, so not that far, as the crow flies."

"You must have seen a bit of the countryside?"

"That's right," Elsie's eyes grew misty with memory. "Charlie often teased me that I had a boy in every town that was sweet on me, but that wasn't true. I only ever had eyes for him. I knew as soon as I clapped my eyes on him that I wanted to marry him. 'Course," Elsie's head rolled against the tree bark as she cast an amused look at Portia, "Father near had a kitten when I told him I was staying put. Charlie and me, we had to marry quick as you like so that Father couldn't cart me off."

"Golly," Portia chuckled. "That sounds all very exciting. Your father must have been sad to lose you to Charlie."

Elsie shrugged. "Angry that he'd have no one to fetch and carry for him, more like. My mother passed when I was still a bairn. Father did marry this harpy, but she didn't like moving from one place to the next. We woke up one morning to find the money tin empty and her clothes all gone. Father wouldn't trust anyone after that."

"Hardly surprising," Portia murmured. She studied the other woman, trying to place her age. "If your father is still alive, could you try and reach out to him now? Send him a letter and explain. I know that travelling fairs and circuses tend to have a base that they use."

"In Staffordshire, yes."

Buoyed, Portia leaned forward. "I'm sure if he

knew the circumstances you were in, he'd want to help."

Elsie shook her head. "He wouldn't. He said that he'd washed his hands of me after I told him I was staying behind with Charlie."

"People say things in the heat of the moment," Portia said gently. "Things that they don't really mean but say to try and hurt the other person."

She shook her head again. "Not my father. He meant it."

"Do you have any other family? A brother or sister? An aunt, perhaps?"

"No. It was always just the two of us. Besides, I have no paper. I haven't written a thing in years."

"I have paper," Portia said. "In my room. You could apply for outdoor relief instead of indoor. A few days to cover your rent. Write to your father. Wait for him to reply."

"And if he doesn't?"

Portia lifted her shoulder, offering the young woman a smile. "You won't know if you don't try. Don't you owe it to Thomas? To know that you exhausted every last avenue available to you before you seek help at the workhouse door?"

Elsie gazed at her. "I think you would have got along with my Charlie. He was always positive, right up to drawing his last breath."

Portia smiled at the compliment. "I'll walk with you to the door, shall I?"

"Very well. It can't hurt, though I can't see that rotter John Cobb giving outdoor relief."

"You know Mr Cobb?"

Elsie snorted. "Only by reputation until today, thankfully."

"I'll be with you," Portia said. She had yet to meet John Cobb in person, though she'd seen him from a distance twice. She knew the reputation the man held locally, and that Elsie was right to be cautious. Damp was seeping into her clothing from sitting on the log and she could only imagine just how cold Elsie was.

The woman clambered unsteadily to her feet, not relinquishing the child despite Portia offering her assistance. The motion seemed to drain her of life and the deep wracking cough that followed made Portia wince.

"Goodness," Portia muttered. "You really shouldn't be out in the rain with that cough."

"I'll be fine enough," Elsie replied.

Portia stepped over the stile, juggling her basket so that she could offer a hand as Elsie carried Thomas over it. Progress was slow, as Elsie had to stop when the cough became too much, yet she was determined enough to get her son out of the drizzling rain. By the time they'd reached the wide oak door of Brookford, the rain was torrential. Portia focused on the task at hand and hurried them both inside.

The chamber was empty, the fire unlit, but the space was dry at least. As Elsie tried to control her coughing, Portia shook the raindrops from her coat.

"We've avoided the Porter. Let me see if I can find someone to help you," Portia said. She stepped into the hallway beyond, but it was empty. She wasn't sure about the admission process – should she let the poor woman further in? Find a fire and some food for her? She dithered in the doorway when footsteps drew her gaze.

"Oh, Mrs Pursley," Portia said with relief as the matron rounded the end of the corridor. "Thank goodness it's you. I'm afraid I –"

"What were you told about using the front door, Miss Summerhill?" The matron demanded sharply. "You cannot dismiss the house rules, simply because it's more convenient for you."

"Someone is seeking outdoor relief, Mrs Pursley. A woman and her child."

"I see," the matron's face had been in shadow as she walked along the hallway but as she reached Portia, she could see her annoyance settled there. "You don't think that we have enough mouths to feed here? You're fetching people in off the street now?"

Elsie's cough filled the room behind Portia and Matron sighed heavily. Portia hoped that the cough was sign enough to the old woman that she'd done the right thing.

"She just needs some money to be able to pay her rent, Mrs Pursley. She was hoping to seek some outdoor relief whilst she waits for her family."

Mrs Pursley studied the scowling Elsie, her eyes running from the exertion of hacking. She drew Portia back out into the hallway, her voice low as she pointed out, "The girl is sick."

"I agree."

"Where did you find her?"

"I heard the child crying," Portia whispered back, not willing to divulge that she'd found poor Elsie in the woods.

"We can't take in just any waif and stray."

"Mrs Pursley, this is the workhouse. We have a duty to those in need. She only needs enough rent for a few days. Outdoor relief will suit her fine. She is going to write to her father –"

"The guardians decide on outdoor relief and those in need. There is a meeting tomorrow. She can come back then."

Portia's lips parted as she realised that the matron was about to put poor Elsie into the rain.

"Mrs Pursley, you yourself said that she's sick. Where's Mr Cobb?"

"Out for the afternoon."

"Mr Finnegan then?"

The matron let her hearty sigh convey just how irritated she was by Portia. "I doubt that the master will be happy to be disturbed by such an event, especially a woman seeking outdoor relief. She'll probably only spend it all on gin anyway. Women like her invariably do."

"She's a widow with a young child. She can't help her circumstances any more than you or I could in that situation. Have a heart, Mrs Pursley," Portia said firmly, though could see that she'd overstepped the mark when the matron's lips pinched white.

"Mrs Pursley?" The deep voice cut through the atmosphere. The outline of William Finnegan was thrown into relief by the lamp that he carried. "Is there a problem?"

Matron Pursley's eyes lit with fervour when she glanced at Portia, knowing that she had her outnumbered now. Matron quickly explained the situation to the workhouse Master, who leaned into the room. He gave a nod when he saw Elsie.

Unfathomable dark eyes settled on Portia, causing a frisson of apprehension to prickle across her skin. "I'll take it from here, Miss Summerhill."

Portia dithered, unwilling to leave the young widow alone with these two as Maisie Milne's words of warning drifted through her inert mind, *People disappear from here all the time.* She'd heard the whisperings throughout the workhouse and, before now, had dismissed it as hearsay. But echoes of a life long ago made her pulse flutter.

She forced a smile to her face. "I've said that I'll help her, Mr Finnegan. I don't mind keeping her company whilst the outdoor relief she's requesting is organised."

Mr Finnegan's smile didn't reach his eyes as he considered her a moment. He turned to the widow. "What is your name?"

"Mrs Elsie Evans."

"Well, Mrs Evans, you're seeking outdoor relief. How many days rent do you require?"

Elsie's eyes darted to Portia. She feared being caught in a lie, and it made her stomach clutch. Elsie had no rooms to pay for – why else had she been seeking indoor relief? The widow would be no good in a poker match. "I am... I had to give up my rooms, sir."

"I see. So why are you seeking outdoor relief when you have no rent payments to meet?"

"Your woman there said that she'd help me reach my father. Course, it might take a while as he's a travelling salesman. I'll write to the lodge he stays at during the slower months.

He won't like it that I'm writing to him. He might not want to save his only daughter from such a fate, but I owe it to Thomas here to try." The cough cut off any more words.

William sighed in irritation. "I'll see to it that she's admitted and taken to the infirmary ward. I don't want her to infect the others with whatever ails her."

"But it might only take a few days to reach her father, Mr Finnegan. Surely outdoor relief is the better option for her –"

His face hardened, his tone stone cold. "Miss Summerhill, I don't believe it is in my job description to have to explain my admission decisions to the likes of you but on this occasion, I will. If we were to hand over money to her now, how long do you think it would be before she was at the door again, asking for more of the same?"

Portia scrambled, trying to apologise, but his furious tirade silenced her. "The money would be squandered. The woman has neither the health nor the ability to be able to earn enough to feed the child, let alone herself when she can barely stand. Indoor relief – whereby she seeks support within the workhouse system, as opposed to outside of it – is the most suitable option here."

"Of course," Portia replied contritely. "I apologise, Mr Finnegan. Thank you for explaining so that I might understand. I promised Mrs Evans that I would help her write to her father. Might I be permitted to speak with her alone a moment?" She would warn her, tell her to wait in the woods once more. Portia would find a way to get out to her tomorrow.

William Finnegan overrode the protests of the matron, his voice stern and low. "Miss Summerhill, offering you this position here was a risk that I was happy to take. Right at this moment, I'm seriously questioning that choice."

Arguing further with them both seemed folly. There was still so much work to be done here, and she'd not nearly scratched the surface of achieving what she'd come here to do.

"I will *handle* this, Miss Summerhill," William grated between clenched teeth.

With one last look at the shivering widow before Matron Pursley chivvied her out of the room and closed the door, Portia wondered if she might have just turned young Thomas into an orphan.

CHAPTER 11

*P*ortia had not known a sleep as restless as last night. The bed felt more like a slab of cold stone than a comfortable place of rest. No matter how many times she turned the pillow, or how she twisted and fidgeted, sleep eluded her. She had picked up a book, attempting to divert her mind, but the words blurred, and all she saw were images of the thin, pale woman huddled under a tree, a crying baby in her arms.

Morning dawned, and the weight of sleep deprivation pressed in on Portia's eyes. In her classroom, her voice wavered as she directed the children through reciting their letters and numbers. She stumbled through the work, her mind miles away, imagining various scenarios involving Mrs Evans. The hours dragged, each tick of the clock pricking her anxiety.

The supper gong's chime was like salvation. Without any delay, she made her way across the yard, barely acknowledging the calls from the children inviting her to join their games, as she headed for the infirmary ward.

She'd not stepped foot in here since the day that the Matron had shown her around Brookford. She knew that she was breaking the rules by opening the door and yet she pushed against it anyway. Inside, the air was a thickly scented mix of ammonia and carbolic soap, used to stave off disease from the unwashed and the decaying.

The elongated room stretched out with rows of iron-framed beds, each holding a weary occupant. The beds were uniformly spaced close together, the straw-filled mattresses offering a scant remedy to any suffering. Drab linen sheets, stained with time and use, covered the inmates, and a thin, scratchy woollen blanket draped over each bed was insufficient against the cold drafts that seeped in from the long windows that lined the one murky beige wall. High ceilings loomed above, intended for ventilation, but all they seemed to do was magnify the room's cavernous feel.

At one end, a fireplace attempted to defy the room's chill, the flames dancing like tormented souls though Portia couldn't feel the heat at this end of the room. A nurse, Agatha, herself an inmate but distinguished by a slightly cleaner apron, stoked the fire, her gaunt face showing the years of hardship etched upon it.

She straightened when she heard the soft click of footsteps on the stone floor, annoyance clear in her eyes. "What are you doing in here?"

"I need to see a woman named Elsie," Portia blurted, side-stepping the nurse, and checking the occupants of the beds. Some lay in listless despair, their eyes vacant. Others coughed weakly; their bodies wracked with pain. A few turned to look at her, hope gleaming faintly in their eyes, searching for any sign of respite or compassion. Portia dismissed each one in her hurry. "She was admitted last night."

"This is my ward," Agatha snapped, eyes narrowed. "You can't just–"

"I have reason to be concerned for her well-being. Please, Agatha, just a moment."

"You shouldn't be in here," Agatha responded with disdain. "I don't poke about in your class-room, do I? Mr Finnegan wouldn't like it either. Does he know you're in here?"

But Portia had spotted the frail figure tucked into a bed near the window. The dim light framed Mrs Evans' pale face, which looked even more gaunt against the white pillow. "There!" Portia exclaimed, pointing, "That's who I mean."

Agatha's voice turned icy. "She's asleep. This isn't a gathering place, Miss Summerhill. Visitors are not permitted without my say-so."

"I'm quite aware," Portia felt a mixture of frustration and relief. "I just needed to know she was okay."

"She's slept all day," Agatha muttered.

"Has she coughed at all?"

Agatha's lips tightened. "You're disturbing my ward, Miss Summerhill. You've seen her now, so, please, leave me to my duties."

Despite Agatha's rebuff, the weight of worry eased from her shoulders. She was filled with quiet gratitude that the widow was at least safe and tended to. Without another word, she nodded, and left the infirmary ward, allowing the door to click softly behind her.

Standing on the step, she took a moment to cast a thankful smile toward the heavens. The ground was still damp from the rain earlier, but now the clouds chased across the sky, allowing the sunlight to peek through. All the worry that had plagued her through the night seemed a little ridiculous now.

"Miss Summerhill!" a child called out, rushing to show her a newly mended stocking. Portia laughed and complimented the child's handiwork. Another approached, displaying his skill with the wooden cup and ball toy for her. "Very good, James," she said, patting his head.

But as she neared the main entrance, she noticed Maisie, usually so vibrant, alone and huddled forlornly in the corner, her dark curls hanging limply around her sad face. "Maisie?" Portia called out to her, but the girl quickly wiped at the tears on her cheeks. Portia approached, her face softening and she gently laid a hand on her thin shoulder. "Maisie, dear, whatever is the matter?"

Maisie blinked, tears glistening on her lashes. "It's Duncan, Miss. They've moved him to the men's yard. I won't see him again."

"Come now," Portia drew the girl close, her heart aching at the plaintive tone.

Duncan Burke had been resistant to any type of education in her classes. He wanted to be outside, working, just as his family had done, and he'd made no bones about this fact. The young girl had spoken often of Duncan and Portia suspected that it was more than a friendship between them both.

"Oh, Maisie, I'm sure it won't be long before you're moved to the women's section. And you'll still get to see him. You've said yourself that you get chosen for the kitchen tasks or emptying the chamber pots because of your hard work. He'll still be here. You shouldn't upset yourself so."

"But Miss, what if they apprentice him out?" Maisie's face crumpled further. "He'll disappear, just like the others."

Portia sighed, brushing away Maisie's tears. "You can't believe everything you hear. These are just tall tales, spun by people to fill their time here."

Maisie looked into Portia's eyes, trying to find the truth. "But why doesn't anyone hear from these people again if they're out there in the world? They don't visit. They don't write. They don't even contact the family that are still in here," her voice was strained as snuffles claimed her once more.

"I...I don't know why," Portia admitted, her voice soft. "Life outside... It's different. Hard. Not everyone has the luxury of free time. Not everyone can write."

"But someone must get a half-day off, right?" Maisie's voice quivered with desperation. "I can't stand the thought of not seeing him again, or knowing what happened to him, Miss. Not Duncan!" Her voice climbed as fear wrapped itself around the words.

She knew that she shouldn't talk about such things with an inmate, but she wanted to offer the young girl some reassurance to ease her pain. "Maisie, I too was taken in by these rumours, about people disappearing just last night. That's all they are – empty whispers and scaremongering." She explained about Mrs Evans, and how the widow was in the infirmary, and that all her worry had been for naught. "I spent a restless night, fretting about Mrs Evans. But today, I saw her with my own eyes, asleep in a bed in the corner."

Maisie eyed her suspiciously, then slowly uttered, "Maybe she's still there because you saw her. Maybe you're a... a what-do-you-call-it?" She searched her mind for the right term. "A witness! That's what kept her from vanishing."

Portia exhaled, her frustration apparent, "Enough of this talk, Maisie. It serves no purpose and only sows fear. Duncan will be fine. He hasn't gone yet and no doubt you'll find a way to visit him during your work. He'll find an apprenticeship on a farm. You'll be taken on one, too, I dare say. A route out of here for you and the chance of a new life."

The child gazed at her, defeated. Portia saw it in the shadows that moved behind her eyes. Maisie might be a young girl, but she'd witnessed much pain and suffering here.

"Yes, Miss Summerhill," she said dully, pushing off from the wall and blending into the throng of children swirling within the walled yard.

Portia watched her, a heaviness in her heart. She'd felt confident that she could make a change here at Brookford, and she'd started to see that within Maisie. She wondered now if she'd lost the girl for good, but how could it serve Maisie to believe the rumours?

Matron Pursley stood in the main entrance, her militant gaze on Portia. Their gazes locked across the yard for a moment, and Portia felt the chill run down her spine. From the way the Matron's eyes narrowed on her, she'd seen Portia with her arm around Maisie and offering the girl comfort. Choosing to avoid a confrontation that would no doubt involve a lecture on being too soft with the inmates, Portia veered away, taking the lesser-used path to the side door.

THE FOLLOWING DAY, the lingering cloud of Mrs Evans' condition pushed Portia to carve out a moment to visit. She had two sheets of paper, her pen and ink well, and an envelope, all tucked in her apron pocket. She had even brought along a slice of bun cake for Agatha to try and grease the wheels of persuading the cranky nurse to allow her to sit with Elsie and write the letter.

Balancing the cake plate in one hand, she knocked and opened the door to the infirmary ward. The dim room was cast in a pallid glow from

the narrow windows. Scents waged war in the air –
the strong, metallic odour of blood, the mustiness
of unwashed bodies, and the slightly sweet, cloying
aroma of decay.

"Good evening, Agatha!" She called out cheerily
into the dreary room though her eyes searched for
Elsie. "I've brought you a little something!"

Today, Agatha was standing at the table that
served as a desk and storage for medicines. Portia
braced herself for the disagreement in the nurse's
gaze as she looked up. "What do *you* want?"

Portia's heart dropped like a stone when she
saw that the bed in the far corner had been
stripped down to the straw mattress, a blanket
folded neatly atop the pillow at the foot of the bed.
"I... I came to check on Mrs Evans," Portia stammered, unease creeping into her voice. "Has she
been moved?"

"Who?"

Portia glanced sharply at the nurse, whose gaze
was fixed on the plate in her hand. "The woman
who was in that bed yesterday. Is she back in the
women's section?"

"She's gone," Agatha responded tersely.

"Gone? Where?"

A dark chuckle escaped Agatha's lips. "She's
dead. Passed in the night."

It was unthinkable. Two days ago, she'd seen

Mrs Evans alive, albeit weak and sickly. Portia's mind raced as she pieced things together, thinking of Maisie's words. She felt as though the ground had given way beneath her, and she clutched the plate tighter, the edges biting into her hand. "How?"

"She was ill," Agatha shrugged as if discussing the weather. "Never even woke up while she was here."

"I see," Portia said, though her mind was reeling. Elsie had been weak, but certainly not on death's door. Maybe she was sicker than she'd realised. Her heart ached for the loss as she set the plate on the table and thanked the nurse. As she turned to leave, another thought occurred to her, "What about her child? Thomas?"

Agatha frowned. "Never saw a child."

Dread pooled in Portia's stomach. Had someone taken Thomas? Was he hidden somewhere, or worse, separated and sent away? "She had an infant son, Agatha. Last I saw him, he was swaddled in blankets."

The raw, vacant look in Agatha's eyes told of the hardened soul beneath. It spoke of a woman who had seen too much and had long ceased to care. "There was no one with her when she arrived. She was much as you saw her yesterday."

"That's impossible," Portia said, frustration

boiling up inside her. She noticed that the nurse's eyes seemed more interested in the extra plate of food rather than the fate of an innocent baby. "She was coughing when she was admitted, yes, but she was lucid. Where would the child be now?" Perhaps the matron had him being cared for by one of the other inmates. Her work was centred around the children – the women fell under the care of Mrs Pursley.

"The workhouse is a big place," Agatha said, her voice dripping with indifference, "Children come and go. Maybe he's been placed somewhere else already. I just do as I'm told. I would advise you to do the same if you know what's good for you."

"Agatha, please," Portia pressed, her voice firm despite the quiver she felt. "I thought that mothers were allowed to remain with the child –"

Agatha's face contorted into a sneer. "I've told you what I know. Now, leave."

Portia turned on a heel and stalked to the door, allowing it to slam behind her. The petty action did nothing to lessen the burden of her tumultuous thoughts. A sick sense of foreboding settled over her.

How could a child just vanish?

Exiting the infirmary, the chilly air outside felt like a slap in the face. Portia's resolve solidified. There were secrets to be uncovered here. She would ensure that Thomas did not vanish into the shadows of the workhouse's cold embrace. She needed answers, and she would not rest until she uncovered the truth.

And she knew exactly where she was going to start looking.

CHAPTER 12

*T*he sewing room was quiet, with only the occasional cough or sigh from the people bent over their work. Maisie worked quickly, her fingers flying over the fabric, her eyes drifting to the window every so often in search of a familiar form.

She had made sure to secure a seat near the grimy window. It allowed her a view of the yard, but the natural light made the position a coveted one by the other women. Maisie had been willing to fight anyone over it, frustrated by the delays that had prevented her from finding a job that allowed her access to the yard sooner, but the atmosphere in the room was more sombre than usual. The brutality from the previous day's events clung to the air, casting a gloomy mood over the brick-lined room.

Edmund Moore's desperate cries during his public whipping by John Cobb had left horrifying images in her mind. The young boy had defied the workhouse rules, escaping from the gardens during work hours, triggering a workhouse lockdown, and likely garnering support from local people as they tried to track him down. Maisie could still see the stark terror in Edmund's eyes when he was hauled back into the building, and she shuddered at the thought of his fate afterwards.

She was almost certain that this was why the women had capitulated to her demands of sitting on the bench nearest the window as soon as Matron had left the room. No one wanted any more trouble today.

Movement caught her eye. Her pulse quickened as men began to file out of their wing, each savouring the fleeting freedom of being outdoors. Maisie pressed her face closer to the glass. As each one emerged, the knots tightened in her stomach. But then, finally, he appeared, sunlight glinting off his hair. Without a second thought, she shot up from her seat, abandoning her sewing, her chair tumbling over and clattering to the stone floor in her haste. Sharp rebukes echoed from the women behind her, voices warning of severe consequences for such insolence. But none of it mattered to her.

Duncan was there. *Alive.*

As Maisie burst into the yard, every eye turned to her. She flew across the yard, everything in her focused on him.

Duncan's face broke into a surprised smile as he caught sight of her. He opened his arms just in time to catch her as she leapt into his embrace. For a moment, all the darkness and cruelty of the past few days melted away, replaced by the warmth of his skin and the roughness of his work clothes. Everything else around her ceased to exist.

"You shouldn't be here, Maisie," Duncan whispered in her ear, though his actions told her that he'd been just as worried about her as she had him.

She pulled back slightly, fingers brushing the scruff on his cheek, sliding around to the hair at the nape of his neck. "I had to see you. I needed to know you were still here."

"Maisie," he murmured, holding her tightly. "It feels so good to see you. But you might get yourself locked in the cupboard again." He gently pushed her away, his fingers linking a moment longer with hers.

Bruises from his beating the other week had faded to yellow. His mouth curved up on one side. "You're staring at me like I'm a just pork steak, girl."

A faint smile wobbled across her mouth. "You're a sight for sore eyes."

"Don't cry," he swiped at the tears that trickled down her cheeks with the pads of his thumbs. "You'll get the stick again."

"I don't care," she grabbed at his hand, needing the contact. "I can't bear the thought of you vanishing."

He squeezed her hand and then stepped back, seemingly self-conscious of the stares that they were drawing from the other occupants of the yard. "I'm fine, Maisie. But you ought to get back in there before anyone sees you. It's tedious enough breaking down those ruddy stones. A man goes near crazy as his mind can't be occupied with the monotony, so he thinks of other things that he has no business to think about. But I don't want to be wondering what happened to you if Matron catches you out here."

"I couldn't care a fig about her," Maisie said even as she cast a look back to the sewing room. From here, she could see the pale faces of the others looming behind the grimy window. "What's been happening to you? Have you heard if you're going to be leaving?"

"No, not yet. Truth be told, there's something amiss. I broke the cardinal rule by not keeping my head down and my mouth shut when I argued with

Cobb the other week. I had a beating, yes. Still, the men here all agree with me that others would have been flogged for less by now. Think about what happened yesterday, right here in this yard."

Instead of easing her worries, his words only grieved her more. "Edmund had the right idea by running away."

Regret pinched Duncan's face. "We heard his shouts from inside. The fool boy was caught on the road. He would have stuck out like a sore thumb on the lanes around here, in his brown clothing, no less."

A reluctant smile tugged at the edges of Maisie's mouth hearing him call Edmund a 'boy'. "He's the same age as you, bar a few months."

Duncan lifted a shoulder. "I'm taller than most in here. But doesn't explain why I didn't get the same treatment as he did."

"It was a terrible scene," Maisie sobered as the memories sloshed against her mind. "I dare say a warning to the rest of us to toe the line."

"You should heed the warning. Go on," Duncan turned her about. "You're pushing your luck being out here. I won't be contained if Cobb takes a whip to you, too."

"I'll try and find you again as soon as I can," Maisie promised. She felt his gaze on her all the way back to the old wooden door to the sewing room.

"Maisie?"

She looked back at him, hope igniting her eyes. "Yes?"

"Will you promise me one thing?"

She cocked her head and smiled. "That depends on what that is."

"I meant what I said. Don't do anything to bring yourself to the attention of John Cobb, you hear? Keep your head down and your nose clean. Promise?"

Across the yard, with the Autumn sunshine lighting the gold in his hair, she felt her heart squeeze at the sight of him. The concern in his eyes made her love him even more. She nodded and then heard the distinct clunk and creak of the main door as it was opened.

She was back at her table, head down and working when Matron Pursley poked her head into the sewing room. The inmates worked silently, and diligently. Maisie waited until the matron had continued on her rounds before she dared to look through the window once more.

Duncan hadn't moved. Through the grubby glass, his image was blurry but when she laid her hand against the cold, smooth surface, he held his hand up to match hers. She remembered the feel of his arms wrapped around her, and she held that assurance close to her.

CHAPTER 13

"*C*ome in."

The door swung open easily and she crept around the edge of the door. Inside, William Finnegan's office was not what she expected. She had envisioned an opulent room to match the stature of the man, but it was anything but. Understated pieces of furniture, white-washed walls, and no ornamental trinkets. It was, in essence, the office of a man who wished to be seen as frugal – or at least, wished for others to believe that of him.

Would a dandy really manage a workhouse? Portia doubted. Considering the horrors that she knew took place under his very roof, she found it hard to believe he wasn't aware. And if he did know, his condonation was equally egregious. She shuddered at the thought.

ANNIE SHIELDS

He looked up, breaking her train of thought. With a chiselled face and piercing dark eyes, he was undeniably handsome, with a veil of enigma adding to his allure. His gaze fixed on her, making her shift on the spot. After what felt like an eternity, he slowly closed the ledger in front of him. His actions felt deliberate, making her discomfort palpable.

"Miss Summerhill," he began in a low, measured tone. "Did you want something?"

Clearing her throat, she fought to keep her voice steady. "Yes, I did, Mr Finnegan."

He pointed at the door with a flick of his hand. "Close the door. Coal costs a fortune, as you will well remember from the meeting you attended, and you're letting cold air in."

She obeyed, biting back a retort about the damp and soiled conditions that the inmates endured daily. She remained standing in the centre of the room, trying to still her hands from pleating the material of her skirt.

He gestured for her to continue, "Get on with it."

"Mrs Evans," Portia said, her voice carrying a hint of hesitation.

The mention of the name seemed to give him pause. For a split second, something flickered across his face. He leaned forward, resting his elbow on the dark wood of his desk. "What about her?"

She mustered her courage. "I believe someone should attend her funeral." The words tripped over themselves in her hurry to explain herself, "I had the privilege of speaking to her before she...passed."

He interjected, "Most unfortunate. But she was very ill."

Portia frowned, "I just think..."

His hand batted the air as if warding off an annoying fly, instead of someone concerned about the death of one of his inmates. "You're too late. The body was collected early yesterday."

"Collected?" she repeated, her voice barely above a whisper, "By whom?"

William Finnegan interlaced his fingers, resting his chin atop them. His gaze was unwavering, stilling her fidgeting. "Miss Summerhill, I don't usually entertain questions from my employees on such matters. But since you seem so vested in this, the body was collected by someone from her parish."

Her eyes narrowed suspiciously, "How very convenient," she murmured.

He leaned back, looking contemplative. "I trust you're not being facetious. Do remember your position here isn't set in stone." He paused for effect. "Besides, I didn't need a corpse rotting here and stinking up the place."

Portia recoiled at his coarseness and the flash of satisfaction in his eyes told her he enjoyed having that effect on her. The power dynamics in the room were clear, and William Finnegan was the puppet master.

The tension in the room thickened, settling heavily around Portia like a musty fur coat. His cavalier attitude stung her. How could anyone speak with such nonchalance about the loss of life? Portia's hand tightened around the fabric of her dress, trying to control the tremors slinking over her skin.

"I wasn't being glib. A woman lost her life, Mr Finnegan," she countered, her voice quivering. "I hope I never come to share such a little regard for another human."

Mr Finnegan raised a brow, the corners of his mouth twisting sardonically. "When you've been associated with workhouses as I have, over the past four decades, you come to appreciate the realities of existence, Miss Summerhill. Life is difficult, and it spares no one. Your dear aunt," he continued, studying her reaction with keen interest, "the one you mentioned with such reverence during your interview, must have done an exemplary job of shielding you from the harsh truths of this world in which we all live."

Portia paled. She had indeed spoken of her aunt during her interview, but she hadn't expected it to be used against her in this manner. Which guardian had divulged those details? Though she'd not said anything confidential, the mere fact that Mr Finnegan held knowledge about a conversation he wasn't part of felt like a violation. She wanted to keep the dear woman's name out of his mouth and away from his attention.

"My aunt might have kept some truths from me, but she also instilled in me a respect for all lives, Mr Finnegan," she straightened, refusing to be cowed by his audacity. "I am quite well-acquainted with life's caprices, too. Now, about Mrs Evans' son, with all the... chaos of the recent incident," she said, alluding to the breakout attempt and the very public punishment of young Edmund, "I haven't had the opportunity to ascertain who has taken up his guardianship. Matron Pursley is always so occupied, so I thought it best to approach you directly, considering you have a hand in every pie."

Mr Finnegan leaned back in his chair, the soft creak of leather the only sound in the oppressive silence that followed. He regarded Portia with an almost predatory gaze, the gleam in his eyes calculating. "I do so hate to be the deliverer of more bad news, Miss Summerhill," he informed her with a sardonic sigh, "but the boy met the same ill fate as his mother."

Portia's heart plummeted. "Both?" she whispered, disbelieving.

He merely nodded, and for a fleeting moment, she thought she saw a glint of perverse joy cross his features. "Indeed."

The stillness that followed was stifling, broken only by the ragged sound of Portia's breaths. She had come looking for answers but had found something far graver. Images of Mrs Evans, with that dark-haired infant cradled to her bosom, scorched Portia's memory. Guilt pressed in on her from all sides. The haunting thought that she might have unknowingly handed them to their doom by bringing them to Brookford consumed her.

Portia tried to swallow; her throat constricted by the storm of emotions. "I-I see," she stammered, struggling to maintain her composure.

"Yes, but all par for the course, Miss Summerhill. We see many sick people through these doors, mostly past the point of being able to help them," Mr Finnegan said, his tone nonchalant. "Will that be all?"

His casual dismissal, as if they were talking about some misplaced item rather than people, infuriated her. She couldn't very well stand in his domain and demand more answers, especially when she knew that none would be forthcoming. Indignation burned her and she welcomed the feeling that soothed the sharp edges of her grief.

"I was wondering if I might request some time off," she asked huskily, emotion stripping her voice raw.

Finnegan glanced up; his gaze sharp. "Out of the question. You had a day the week before last."

"Mr Finnegan, my agreement with the guardians was half a day a week," she said, trying to maintain her ground. "Even the inmates get a Sunday off."

His lip curled, a shadow of a sneer playing at the corner of his mouth. "Am I mistaken, Miss Summerhill, or were you not at the guardian's meeting three months ago, bemoaning the fact that you had an overwhelming amount to do? Too many children to fit into your class in one go, I believe you said."

Heat scorched Portia's cheeks. Still, she held her ground as his tirade continued.

"And did you not beg for more teaching materials with which to enlighten the children? At a great deal of expense to us, I hasten to add.

Perhaps you should spend your time acquainting the children with them instead of seeking leisure," his gaze bored into her, almost daring her to challenge him further. "That would be best, don't you agree?"

She took a breath, attempting to articulate her thoughts. "Mr. Finnegan, I—"

"If that will be all," he interrupted, his tone dripping with condescension. Picking up his pen, he dipped it into the inkwell. He flipped open the ledger, his focus shifted entirely to his work. "I'm busy," he muttered, not looking up.

Portia moved towards the door; her footsteps heavy. She felt the weight of his gaze on her back. The knowledge that Mrs Evans had met her end within these walls, combined with the tales she'd heard from Maisie about people mysteriously disappearing, sent shivers down her spine. But it was the realisation of her own confinement, of her inability to verify the truth beyond these walls, that left her truly shaken. At the threshold, she paused, turning for one last appeal.

The low light filtering in through the dusty windows highlighted the furrowed lines on William's face as he met Portia's tormented gaze.

"What is it?" he demanded.

"The body was picked up?" she asked. "Does that mean someone reached her father?"

"Her what?" His dark eyes narrowed with suspicion.

"Mrs Evans mentioned she was going to ask her father for help, which tells me she had a family who would miss her," Portia elaborated, trying to piece together the events leading to the poor woman's demise, her heart thudding loudly against her ribcage. "I was thinking that if her father was able to claim her body, the sad news would be easier to digest. You said that her body was claimed."

William's tone dripped with disdain. "No, the body was collected by the undertaker's subcontractor, Miss Summerhill."

"Bodies," Portia corrected him.

He paused, eyes averted, before mumbling, "That's right. Bodies."

THE SILENCE STRETCHED ON, heavy with implications. Portia's mind raced, grasping at every detail. With every ounce of mettle she could drag up, Portia asked, "What parish was he from?"

The pen made a plopping sound as he dropped it on the ledger. He didn't seem to notice that splash of ink it made in his book. A muscle bounced in his jaw. It was all she could do not to retreat. "What's it to you?"

Forcing a sad smile, she replied, "The thought of

someone as full of life as Mrs. Evans was being buried in an unmarked grave, without any mourners... It's heart-wrenching. I'd like to pay my respects and lay a posy on her final resting place."

William's laughter held no warmth. "Well, seeing as it will be a pauper's burial, there'll more than likely be several of them going into the same grave. And it won't be marked, Miss Summerhill. I'd save your sentiment for where it's deserved."

"What parish was the undertaker from, Mr Finnegan?"

Too late, she realised her mistake. Portia had hoped to catch him in a lie. Mrs Evans had told her where her father lived. A parish would have to meet the cost of the burial so that Brookford wouldn't have to. The workhouse served a great many communities and parishes locally, but what were the odds that an undertaker collecting another pauper from the same parish was here at the same time? There was no way that she could prove that the widow had indeed ended up buried back in her hometown.

His smile, if it could be called that, was one of a predator catching his prey off-guard. "Staffordshire, Miss Summerhill. I believe a place called Longnor."

Of course, a man like William Finnegan was too smart to be caught that easily. She exited the room;

the burden of knowledge battered her senses. Mrs Evans's death, Maisie's whispered warnings, the mysterious disappearances — all seemed to form a web of deceit and darkness that she was stuck in. She was in the lion's den, and now the lion would be watching her every move.

CHAPTER 14

*M*aisie didn't mind being in the laundry room on days like today. At least she was warmer in here than sitting in the hall on the stone floor picking oakum. The sky was the kind of blue that stung the eyes and the nip in the air warned that shorter winter days were on the way.

The laundry room was bigger than the other working rooms, filled with rows upon rows of large wooden barrels, each brimming with cloudy, soapy water. Nearby, large vats of boiling water bubbled and fussed, steam rising in serpentine tendrils towards the ceiling, forming a stifling, humid atmosphere that hazed the windows. Stone floors bore evidence of water and soap suds that had sloshed over the sides of the basins lining the opposite wall, mingling with the dirt and grime that had been scrubbed off countless workhouse garments.

The perpetual wetness made the coarse material of Maisie's uniform stick to her skin as she wrung out the sodden masses of clothing.

Lines of tautly stretched rope crisscrossed the ceiling, and a large wooden contraption attached to one wall allowed for row upon row of clothing to be strung along the bars that would raise and lower by a series of pulleys.

In the centre of the room stood heavy, cast-iron mangles. Each mangle was manned by a grim-faced woman, turning the massive handles, squeezing every drop of water out of the washed items before dropping them into a basket for another woman to hang up and dry. The rhythmic creaking of the mangles and the methodical sloshing of water offered a droning backdrop to the otherwise muted hum of the room.

Amidst the steam and sweat, Maisie enjoyed the work. Although the soap suds caused her hands to become chapped and raw as she scrubbed, rinsed, and wrung out garments, time always passed by quickly.

As with all the other rooms in the workhouse, one inmate took responsibility for the workload. Betty Shaw had come from London. She would tell stories about her times as a housemaid in Bayswater and Bethnal Green before she'd married a blacksmith. The local man had been a cad, with a roving eye, according to the tales, but Betty had loved him anyway.

The thick, heavy mist formed a veil on the comings and goings of those who entered the laundry room. Engrossed in her task, Maisie's focus was unwavering, her fingers deftly agitating the striped bedding to ensure every last louse was dislodged. Ethel Crabtree, a seasoned worker with a keen eye for everything, nudged her slightly. Maisie's eyes followed Ethel's subtle nod.

Duncan stood, amidst the linens, drawing a mix of shock and disapproval from the women present over the daring trespass. Dripping cloth forgotten, Maisie started toward him. She watched as Duncan, with a roguish twinkle in his eyes, tried to placate Betty, whose face showed clear disapproval. When he caught sight of her weaving her way through the baskets and women, his eyes lit up and he whipped off his cap, holding it against his chest.

"You're not supposed to be in here," Betty huffed, hands on her hips.

"I know, I know," he admitted, that irresistible grin never leaving his face. "But some things are worth breaking the rules for."

Betty's stern expression melted a touch at

Duncan's charm. She cast a worried glance around the room. "If Matron sees you in here, we'll all be done for!" she warned, her voice trailing off, envisioning the potential repercussions.

Duncan cocked his head, a cheeky wink softening her more. "If she comes in, I'll say I forced you to let me in. Blame me."

Betty sighed, relenting. "A few minutes. Not a moment more."

Nodding his appreciation, Duncan pulled Maisie into the corner, away from the door. The murmurs and stares of the other women reached her ears, but as Duncan positioned himself protectively in front of her, they seemed to fade away.

He filled her version. She looked up into his face and it was only then that she noticed the playfulness with which he'd charmed his way into the room with Betty had vanished, replaced with a more serious look that sent shivers down her spine.

"What's wrong?"

Without a preamble, he said, "Arthur Strong is back here, and he has some stories to tell. It's Arthur, so we're not sure whether to believe him or not."

Maisie's brow furrowed. Arthur Strong was one of those inmates who flitted in and out of the workhouse according to his mood and his luck in the gambling halls.

"What stories?"

"Do you remember Sallie Bell?"

She nodded, her heart fluttering. Sallie had been apprenticed into service in the spring of the previous year. She'd been bragging about it for days leading up to her leaving, about how she was going to earn money and buy a fancy dress so that she'd never have to wear the rotten brown uniform ever again.

She'd not been heard from since.

Duncan hesitated and dread turned her legs to lead. "Arthur saw her."

Maisie's frown deepened. "Well, that's good news, isn't it? That she's alive and well although..." She thought about the types of places that Arthur Strong claimed to frequent. "Where did he see her?"

"Not in any fine house that she was meant to be cleaning, that's for certain," Duncan glanced back. As predicted, the women were feigning the work and so he leaned down, his mouth next to her ear, and whispered, "It was the kind of place where fallen women go to work."

He straightened up but she shook her head, still none the wiser. "Where?"

He leaned down again, "He was in a bordello on Mardol, in Shrewsbury, Maisie. Sallie is a dollymop."

Maisie reared back, eyes wide in horror. "A prostitute?"

Duncan winced and quickly laid a finger against his lips. "Yes," he hissed, patting the air to remind her to keep her voice low. "Arthur spoke tried to speak to her, but she ran away from him."

"Poor Sallie," she murmured, "I can't imagine what happened to her to force her into a life such as that."

"That's the thing," Duncan's eyes shone with fervour. "Arthur reckons the abbess – the woman who is in charge there," he explained when she shrugged over the word, "She told him that Sallie had never been in service, though she liked to tell people she was meant to be. She'd arrived there via a different place, a place that they called The Court. There was a whole covey of women there who confirmed it to him when he checked."

"I don't know what you're trying to tell me," Maisie said when he stared at her, as though he was willing her to understand. "What's The Court?"

"It sounds as if it is a place that trades girls, Maisie. Women who've come straight from work-houses like this one."

Maisie blinked, her mind stumbling as the shock of his words settled in her mind. "Do you think that that's what has been happening to the girls who have been apprenticed out?"

"Orphans, Maisie. Girls who won't have a family to miss them."

Maisie swallowed; her mouth suddenly dry. *Orphans like her.* "I don't – I can't... we have to tell someone."

Duncan spread his hands. "Who will believe us? All the men are dismissing Arthur's stories as just that – stories. Fibs made up, but Sallie left before he was here last year. He knew who she was, of course –"

"But not that she'd gone into service," she finished.

He laid his hands on her shoulders, his grip tight as he gave her a gentle shake. "You cannot let them move you into the women's section."

Maisie's smile was sad, and she lifted a hand to stroke his cheek. "It's not as if I would have much choice, is it? I will have to go where they put me."

"No," Duncan said. "I'll find a way to get us out of here. I promise."

"I know you mean it, but you can't keep a promise like that," she said gently.

"That's long enough," Betty's voice was low and urgent. "I said a few minutes and you're pushing your luck now, young Burke."

Duncan's eyes didn't leave Maisie's. He caught her hand and squeezed before he dipped his head and kissed her cheek. Then he was gone, striding through the misty room.

"Are you alright, girl? You look a bit peaky," Betty asked her quietly.

Maisie's smile was brief. She couldn't repeat what Duncan had said. The women here were already on tenterhooks over all the changes. But before Maisie could say anything, Nellie Jones' complaining voice cut through the steam. "How is it that she is allowed visitors in here? What's so special about her?"

Betty snorted. "Your beau wouldn't lower himself to come into a place like this."

"He ain't my beau," Nellie replied slowly, though the accompanying smile exposed her lie.

"Then why do you keep asking to see him, Nellie?" Ethel Crabtree muttered. "I wouldn't mind if I never had to see his ugly fizzog again."

Nellie's smile grew. "He says he wants to marry me."

Betty barked out mirthless laughter. "Well, you're making a deal with the devil, Nellie, and I don't mind telling you that."

Maisie made her way back to her barrel, giving a little nod when Ethel nudged her, wordlessly asking if she was okay.

"Maybe I'll tell John that we had a little visitor

in here today," Nellie taunted, a malevolent light lighting up her pretty eyes.

Maisie whirled on her, snatching up a washing dolly. She brandished it as she charged across the room, yelling at Nellie.

Nellie flattened herself against the wall. "Get away from me, ya fiend!"

"You breathe a word and I'll wipe that smile right off your face, Nellie Jones!" The fear of what John Cobb would do to Duncan sent fear zipping along her veins. John Cobb didn't need much of an excuse to dole out punishment.

"I won't say a word, just get away from me!"

"What on *earth* is going on in here? I can hear the racket on the other side of the yard! The men are meant to be exercising, not listening to a bunch of banshees!" Matron Pursley's voice sliced through the room, cutting the noise and chatter to silence, but the fury was still pumping through Maisie's veins. She bared her teeth at Nellie.

"Maisie! Drop that at once!"

Reluctantly, Maisie set the wooden equipment down. Even as Matron was dragging her from the room, Maisie didn't take her eyes off the snivelling Nellie.

CHAPTER 15

*P*ortia found the very idea of a social event within the workhouse indecorous and, at first, she declined the offer, much to the disgust of Mrs Pursley.

To her, a hearty meal with wine felt inappropriate when people were living on gruel and thinned stew only a few feet away. When Portia had questioned the morality of it though, Matron had told her that it was an annual event whereby the Board of Guardians gathered to enjoy the fruits of the workhouse gardens that had been harvested and prepared by the inmates and that attendance was obligatory unless she wished to find work elsewhere.

The hall was abuzz with the gentle hum of conversation. Polished silverware gleamed under the golden light of the gas lamps, and the heady aroma of the harvest feast filled the room. Freshly picked fruits, glistening joints of meat, and loaves of bread were laid out in a decadent display of abundance. The irony wasn't lost on Portia: such opulence was a stark contrast to the sparse meals the inmates consumed.

Mrs Draper, with her fluttery hands and nervous fidgeting, was animatedly discussing the latest London fashions, while Mr White, the local banker with a sharp wit, engaged in a heated debate about the economy with his peers. Portia felt like a bird in a gilded cage as she was introduced to the guardians she'd not yet met, and she was greeted with varying degrees of suspicion and pity. She was desperate to seize an opportunity to speak privately to those she considered allies, wanting to air the concerns that plagued her during the long nights here, but the room's confined space made any covert discussions a near impossibility.

However, Portia soon recognised a potential silver lining. With most of the staff preoccupied in here, she could perhaps utilise this time to gather some intelligence or maybe even find some tangible evidence. She listened with half an ear to Mrs Draper's inquiries about the children's education and Mr Simmons' concerns about their health.

Their genuine concern was a balm to her heart.

But even that comfort was marred by the constant sensation of being watched.

John Cobb.

For months, she'd avoided the workhouse porter. Their duties didn't intermingle, and she thanked her lucky stars that this was the case. He sat at the far end of the room, cutting a solitary figure. He had receding brown hair and the air of a man used to being obeyed. She hadn't seen him smile once and it seemed to her almost as if the guardians circumvented him.

His icy blue eyes, cold and penetrating, seemed to follow her every move. She'd felt the weight of his stare as soon as the introductions were being made around the table. The intensity of his scrutiny set her on edge.

Ensuring that many of the board members were engrossed in their plates and conversations, Portia excused herself, hoping to slip away unnoticed. But as she rose, John Cobb was suddenly beside her, his tall frame casting a shadow over her petite stature.

"I know you, don't I?" His voice was deep, filled with an unsettling familiarity.

Caught off-guard, Portia had to force her frozen lips to move into a smile she was far from feeling. She gave a slight shake of her head and said, "I'm sure I'd remember meeting you."

Cobb leaned in, searching her face as if trying to

decipher a puzzle. The faint smell of tobacco and brandy laced his breath, "Oh, I'm certain we've crossed paths. One way or another."

She wanted to lean back, out of the way of him, unnerved by the way his eyes narrowed in his study of her. "I'm sorry, Mr Cobb–" she began.

"You look familiar to me," he stated, in an almost accusatory manner.

She blinked owlishly at him, feigning surprise. "Do I?"

"Where are you from?"

"Berkshire," she replied, hoping her voice wouldn't betray her apprehension. "I grew up there with an aunt."

"Your parents were from there?" He pressed, suspicion edging his voice.

Before she could answer, the sound of a chair scraping against the floor caught their attention. Reverend James stood tall at the head of the table. "Ladies and gentlemen, if I may," he began, causing conversations to halt and heads to turn in his direction, "let us bow our heads in gratitude and prayer, to thank the Lord for the bounties before us."

Portia eagerly welcomed the interruption. As everyone lowered their heads, Reverend James continued, "We give thanks for this food and to the hands that have prepared it. And for the staff, who, with selfless devotion, care for the poor."

As heads bowed and murmurs of prayer filled the room, Portia seized her opportunity. She subtly edged towards the door. By the time the room reverberated with a collective "Amen," John Cobb had vanished.

Confused but grateful for his sudden absence, she slipped through the door, praying that she wouldn't bump into him in the corridor if he was returning from a natural break.

The reverberations of the ongoing celebration became muffled as she ventured further into the winding corridors of the workhouse. Clutching her candle, Portia made her way towards the work-house master's office, the flickering flame causing the whitewashed walls to dance with sinister shadows.

With every step, her pulse quickened. As she reached the door, she hesitated, listening for any signs of movement. Silence greeted her. Taking a deep breath, she quietly turned the knob, unsur-prised at the arrogance of the workhouse master for leaving it unlocked.

The scent of Macassar oil lingered in William's office, and she knew that he must use the product in his hair. The soft glow of her candlelight illuminated the ruthlessly uncluttered room. For a moment, the corners of the room moved with the low light, causing her heart to stutter in her chest. Terror filled her. What would happen to her if she was caught in here snooping? She drew in a bracing breath and quickly crossed to the wide desk, her eyes scanning for the distinctive burgundy ledger with its gold filigree pattern. She hoped it held the key to understanding what really went on behind these walls.

She opened and closed the drawers, finding the ledger in the bottom one. With trembling fingers, Portia withdrew it and set it on the desktop. The weight of its thick pages and leather-bound cover was evident as she held it. Flicking it open, her eyes danced over the meticulous handwritten records. Her guess had been right. This ledger held names, dates, admissions, deaths, and discharges, all recorded in William Finnegan's immaculate hand.

She moved the candle closer as she frantically searched for the date she knew so well because it haunted her dreams - the date Elsie and little Thomas were brought into the workhouse.

As the minutes passed, her desperation grew. Alarm welled in her chest as she moved back and forth between the pages. She'd let them into the workhouse herself. Had seen Elsie in a workhouse bed in the infirmary. She'd wanted to see what the cause of their death had been recorded as. Yet, according to this ledger, Elsie and Thomas had never stepped foot in this place. A chill ran down her spine.

She straightened up. Was it negligence? An oversight? But she couldn't see a man as calculating as William Finnegan making such a grave mistake, especially since she'd raised the questions about Elsie. Doing this would have reminded him about the widow, surely?

Standing there, she stared at the page where their names should have been lodged. This was her proof that he'd been remiss in his work, but it didn't prove anything more sinister. She wanted to take the ledger with her, but Mr Finnegan would notice such a thing missing immediately.

Suddenly, the faint echo of footsteps reached her ears, reminding her of the peril she was in being in here in the first place. She hastily closed the ledger and slid it back into its hiding spot. Dousing the candle and plunging the room into darkness, she used the moonlight streaming through the window to edge her way to the door. Quiet as a church mouse, she cracked open the door to check the corridor was empty. It was the soft laugh, throaty and low, that froze her to the spot.

A woman's laugh. Was it one of the guardians?

She ducked back into the master's office, waiting, blood thundering in her ears, but no one came. Quelling her ragged breathing as much as she could, she listened. No more footsteps, but she was certain that she could hear the hushed rumble of voices. Torn, she hovered, the door slightly open. A static light illuminated the corner that she needed to escape through. She waited a moment more before she slipped through the door. Her hand on the door handle, she concentrated on closing the door as quietly as possible when the scrape of a boot on the stone floor behind her squeezed out a yelp.

"Miss Summerhill?" John Cobb's voice dripped with amused malice. "What a surprise to find you here, sneaking around outside the workhouse master's office."

"Not at all, Mr Cobb," she replied, grateful that she'd left the ledger where she'd found it. "I was looking for him actually."

He took his time reaching for the oil lamp high up on the wall as if to illustrate the fact that the candle dish she clutched was unlit. "In the dark? Surely, he was in the hall with the rest of the staff and guardians."

She waited as he lit the candle for her, murmuring her thanks. "You're right."

His eyes gleamed in the light as he shifted his

attention back to her. "What did you need to speak to Billy about?"

It was jarring hearing him speak in such a familiar manner about his employer. As much as she disliked William Finnegan, the familiarity seemed disrespectful. "I have misplaced a shawl. I was going to ask him if he'd found it, or if an inmate had handed it in."

He tilted her chin up, forcing her to meet his gaze. The closeness made her uncomfortable, the weight of the ledger's secrets pressing heavily upon her. "You're a poor liar, Miss Summerhill," he whispered, a hint of a threat lurking in his tone.

Her skin burned where his fingers gripped her, and terror had her twisting out of his grip. She swallowed hard, even as her mind was racing with trying to come up with a way of extricating herself from this situation safely. "I don't know what you're implying, Mr Cobb."

His mouth twisted as he pretended to consider her lie though the movement at the end of the corridor caused her to swing, bracing herself for what was to come next. It took a few moments for her eyes to adjust to the sight of a pretty, dishevelled young woman, her cheeks flushed and her full lips still wet.

"Nellie Jones?" Portia's voice echoed slightly as she

stepped a little closer to her. The woman moved in the light. Portia saw the glint in the younger woman's eyes, a potent mixture of mischief and gratification and she realised that she had found the source of the throaty laughter she'd heard just moments before. "Why are you out here and not in your dormitory?"

"I will handle this," John Cobb pushed Portia out of the way. In the lamplight, she saw how his face reddened.

Nellie, casting a sideways, almost flirtatious glance at John, replied, "There's no harm done, Miss. We were just... talking."

She tilted her head to look at Nellie again, noticing the way her eyes lingered on Cobb and the subtle smirk that played on her lips. Comprehension dawned. There was more going on here than met the eye. John Cobb's tall frame moved to obstruct Portia's view, his expression dark.

"This doesn't concern you," he snapped at Portia.

Nellie's unexpected appearance had given Portia a momentary advantage. She now had a secret about the workhouse porter, one that might ensure that he held his tongue over finding her leaving the workhouse master's office.

She decided to use it. "Perhaps not," she replied with a curt nod, her voice cold. "But it's curious, isn't it? What would the guardians think, I wonder, of such goings-on in the workhouse?"

His face was a picture of fury and humiliation. "You will not speak of this," he warned, his voice low and dangerous.

Portia's lips curled in a slight smile. "Oh, Mr Cobb, I think we understand each other quite well now, don't we? Your secret is safe with me."

She didn't wait for a response. Whirling around with a flourish of her skirts, Portia made her way back to the gathering. The muted sounds of chatter and laughter from the party were a stark contrast to the tension she left behind in the corridor,

Reverend James was holding court, regaling a group with tales of a recent trip to London. Portia tried to slip in unnoticed, but Mrs Draper caught sight of her.

"Ah, Miss Summerhill! We thought you'd left the festivities," she said jovially.

She smiled, the movement stiff, her mind whirling with all that she'd discovered. Nellie's presence outside the workhouse master's office added another layer of complexity she hadn't anticipated. "Just needed some fresh air, that's all."

She nodded understandingly. "This hall can get quite stifling, especially with so many of us gathered. Tell me, what do you think of Gladstone's latest reforms?"

William Finnegan glanced at her from near the fireplace then back at his mentor. Portia released the breath that she'd been holding, relief flooding her. She'd managed to escape John Cobb's scrutiny for now, but she did not doubt that he would be watching her closely from here on. Still, she took solace in the fact that she now had something to hold over him — a secret that might just keep her safe. She was playing a dangerous game, but the stakes were too high to back down now.

Tonight, at least, Portia had the upper hand.

CHAPTER 16

*I*t took Portia a moment to realise that the sharp drumming sound wasn't a dream. She wasn't being chased along endless corridors by a faceless creature. Someone was at her door.

The pounding continued, yanking her from sleep. Groggily, she slipped from her bed, disorientated. Weak morning light threw the treeline into prominence, but it was still too dark to see anything more from her bedroom window. She found her shawl, swinging it over her shoulders as the knocking continued, more urgent.

Matron Pursley stood on the other side of the door, her nightdress askew, her greying plait over one shoulder. There was no mistaking the alarm carved into her face.

"What is it?" Portia asked though the sleepiness that had clouded her mind evaporated instantly, her senses assaulted. Through the floors, deep in the belly of the building, she heard the commotion.

Worse, she could smell the smoke.

"There's a fire – you must come."

Her thoughts went immediately to the children, the elderly, and those who might need assistance with the steep stairs. Portia snatched up her lamp, dragging the edges of her shawl closer as she hurried after Matron. As they descended the staircase, the smoke grew thicker, making it difficult to see and breathe. A cacophony of shouts echoed, panic-filled voices, and bellows boomed as they entered the chaos.

"Everybody out!"

"All hands on deck!"

"Not that door – the other one!"

In the hallway, the men had formed a chain, ferrying buckets from the well outside. Shouts of the fire marshal and his deputies, defined by their blue woollen tunics and helmets, penetrated the cloying air. Unable to hold her breath, Portia started to cough, eyes burning.

"Miss! Miss!" One of the deputies was snapping his fingers at her. "The children! Take them outside!" He followed the direction of his pointing finger, and she spotted a small cohort – some crying, some with vacant looks on their faces – lingering on the staircase. It was the small hand slipping into hers that grounded her.

She looked down and recognised Andrew, a bright boy with a gift for numbers, gazing up at her with complete trust. Feeling along the walls, she made her way through the pandemonium, gulping in deep lungfuls of clean, fresh air as she emerged from the building.

"Wait here, Andrew," she instructed him. "You're in charge. I'm relying on you to make sure everyone stays here, outside, and out of the way. Count them and remember the number."

His dark head nodded, and she turned to go back inside.

"Where are you going?" Matron Pursley stopped her.

Portia looked down at the hand that bit into her forearm. "To get the others," Portia replied as if the response was obvious.

"Don't be absurd," Matron replied. "The firemen are dealing with it. We are to wait here."

Horrified, Portia looked at the building. Smoke billowed steadily from the lower floor window; the white façade scorched black as though licked by the devil himself. Portia stared at the damage, even as the children pressed closer to her legs. The window she'd looked through last night when she'd snuck in there.

William Finnegan's office was on fire.

She thought about the children she'd just led from there, scared and cowering on the stairs. She thought about how scared she would have been in the same situation. She thought about those sweet faces, locked away night after night…

Portia tightened her shawl around her face, bracing herself for another trek through the suffo- cating haze. As she entered the hallway, she could barely make out the frantic movements of fire- fighters and inmates, their shouts a cacophonous medley amidst the roaring fire.

On her second trip into the smoke-filled corri- dors, Portia heard a distinct voice piercing through the din. It was Maisie, her tone tinged with desperation.

"Duncan, please! We must go!"

Portia followed the sound, her eyes tearing up from the smoke. She found them: Maisie pulling at Duncan's arm, as he was trying to douse the flames with a bucket of water.

"Miss Summerhill, please," Duncan's voice was firm, even through the pandemonium. "Take her to safety."

Portia reached out and grasped Maisie's arm,

trying to offer some semblance of comfort. "Maisie, come with me. We need your help!"

"But Duncan–"

"There are children trapped on the stairs; they're too scared to move and it's too dark to see the way out. We need to guide them out."

Duncan met Maisie's gaze, determination and concern battling in his eyes. "Go with her, I'll be fine. I promise. Right now, those children need you."

Maisie hesitated, her eyes flicking back and forth between Duncan and Portia. The seconds felt like hours. Finally, she nodded, swallowing hard. "Alright. Let's go."

Armed with sheer determination and adrenaline, Portia and Maisie navigated through the smoky maze, hacking, and coughing but pushing forward. Reaching the staircase, they found the group of frightened children, bunched together, their faces tear-streaked and smudged with soot.

"It's alright, we're here to take you outside," Maisie assured them, her voice surprisingly steady.

Taking the lead, Portia signalled for the children to form a line. "Hold each other's hands. Don't let go, no matter what."

One by one, with Maisie guiding from the back and Portia leading the way, they ushered the children down the stairs and along the chaotic hallway.

Finally, they stumbled through the entrance and burst out into the night air.

Three more times she did this, herding inmates and children out, until Andrew confirmed that she had all her youngsters standing in the yard. They huddled in wild-eyed clusters, shivering in the dawn light.

Portia felt a hand on her arm, and she turned to see John Cobb this time, his face blackened with soot, but his eyes clear and determined. "Have you seen Nellie?" he asked, his voice raw.

Portia shook her head, the chaos around them making it difficult to think. "No, I haven't, but some of the inmates took the other stairs, according to one of the firemen. We ought to do a head count..."

But he was already moving away from her, plunging into the swarming group, shoving men and women out of his way. She tracked his movements, her line of sight drawn to where the efforts seemed most concentrated. People eddied around her as she stared at the gaping void of the office.

Daylight had turned the sky to a pale grey by the time the firemen had declared the fire extinguished.

"It's safe?" Portia asked the man.

He glanced at her briefly then took a closer look. "It is, miss. You the one who came back for the nippers?"

"That's right."

Admiration moved his head, and he nodded once. "By my eye, you did them a good turn. Better than that other old crone. She could eat vinegar with a fork, that one."

Portia tried to hide her smile. Matron Pursley could be sharp with the inmates. Clearly, outside of the workhouse, people didn't appreciate her tone. "She was probably scared."

The fireman harrumphed. "Don't know why – I explained to her that the fire was contained to the main office only. We had them remove everyone as a precaution only."

"Just the office?" Portia asked. "There was so much smoke."

"That's right, miss. Smoke can be deadlier than fire sometimes, but I would say that the response from your residents here saved the day.

Mr Finnegan said he was straightening up when he noticed that a candle had fallen over. He went to fetch some water but by the time he returned, the curtains had ignited. These things have a habit of getting out of control very quickly. Luckily, he was awake, else it could have been worse."

"Indeed, Mr Benson."

They both turned to look at the richly deep voice standing behind them. The fireman recovered first. "Ah, Mr Finnegan, there you are, sir. I was just explaining to the young woman here that the fire is contained."

"Good news, I must say." William nodded, his dark eyes scanning the damage. "Please pass along my thanks to your crew. I've had the cook prepare some food and tea for you all."

"Very kind, sir, but we'll be on our way if it's all the same to you. But before I go," Mr Benson indicated to Portia. "Your woman here ought to be commended on her brave actions. She did you proud tonight, Mr Finnegan."

Portia suppressed a shiver when the dark gaze settled on hers. "We're very lucky to have her, Mr Benson."

"I'll be off then."

Portia watched as the fireman rounded up his crew. Through the gloom, she spotted John Cobb with Nellie Jones. William Finnegan had seen the pair, too. She turned to the workhouse master and asked, "Is there much damage?"

"It's too soon to tell," he replied. His eyes lingered a moment longer on the couple and then he turned the full force of his shuttered stare on her. "The fire started in the desk though, as that's where I was sitting."

Fear turned her blood to ice.

"All of that damage because I was careless. The desk is most certainly ruined," he said quietly, calmly, as if telling her about the weather. "No doubt other... records have gone up in smoke, too."

She caught the malevolent glint in his eyes, and she swallowed, trying to unstick her tongue from the roof of her mouth. She was almost certain that he knew that she'd been snooping in his office, that she was aware he'd not written either Elsie's or Thomas' names in his ledger. Of course, a fire was a convenient reason for his records to be destroyed.

All that evidence... Gone.

"H-how terrible for you."

His mouth twisted and, for a moment, she felt as if she was peering into an abyss, with danger shimmering all around her. When he broke the trance to look up at the building's façade, she followed his gaze. He lifted a nonchalant shoulder, shooting the cuffs on his shirt. "That's the thing about this workhouse, Portia," he murmured, low enough that it was meant only for her ears. "Careless accidents can happen."

She watched him walk away. He stalked through the crowd, flicking a hand at John Cobb, who then began to organise the inmates. The workhouse master cut a grandiose figure amongst the sea of drab brown uniforms. A master, indeed, of all that he surveyed.

Accidents happen.

A shiver stole over her, and she wrapped the

shawl closer when she remembered another accident that had happened here not so long ago.

The one where the master's wife was found at the foot of the wrong staircase in the middle of the night.

CHAPTER 17

"$\mathcal{M}$iss Summerhill?"

Portia jolted at the softly tentative voice. She looked up sharply, astonished to see Maisie Milne in her schoolroom. She'd not even heard her come in.

"How long have you been standing there?"

"I did knock," Maisie said hastily, her eyes darting to the open doorway at her back. "I shouldn't have bothered you."

Portia shook her head. She quickly folded the letter that had engrossed her so and tucked it into the pocket of her apron, beckoning the girl forth as she dallied in the doorway. "It's fine, Maisie. Did you want something?" Still, the girl hesitated. Portia released a soft sigh, and moderated her tone more, digging deep to try and find a smile. It wasn't right that she took out her foul temper on the poor girl. "Please, come in. How are you after last night?"

"I can still smell smoke," Maisie replied with a wrinkled nose, pulling at a hank of her hair. "We are not allowed to walk through the building, either. We have to go around the outside, so that's a nice change, even if it is piddling down."

Portia suppressed a smile at the coarse language. "A welcome change, indeed."

Maisie checked the hallway behind her and pushed the door shut. "Duncan says I'm wasting my time for saying something but I... I think someone should know. Not that you'll know what to do. You might not want to know, as it is but I think someone ought to know–"

Portia's brows met and she held her hands out in front of her to stem the torrent of words. "Maisie – slow down. What are you talking about?"

Maisie chewed her lip, her hands in knots in front of her. "Duncan said..." The girl clamped her mouth shut, rolling her lips inwards as she debated with herself. Portia remained silently still, waiting for Maisie to summon her courage, even as her thoughts ran amok. "Do you know Arthur Strong?"

Portia had a vague image of an inmate: a tall, thin man with dark, stringy hair and wily eyes as if he were someone used to looking over his shoulder. "Yes, is he the man that's recently taken indoor relief?"

"That's him," Maisie nodded, taking another step into the room. "He's telling stories now that probably can't be believed."

Portia frowned, trying to decipher her sentence structure.

"Except," Maisie continued, "he wasn't here when Sallie Bell left."

"Maisie," Portia remarked as patiently as she could, "you're talking in riddles."

Anguish evident in her voice, Maisie threw her hands wide. "She's a prostitute, miss! She was meant to have been apprenticed out as a maid in a decent house. Instead, she was taken away to a place in the city. She told Arthur Strong that she was sold to the highest bidder, and now she lives in a brothel on Shrewsbury."

Portia studied Maisie. A small part of her mind - the logical part - hoped that Maisie's story was just that: a fantastical tale woven by an idle mind. But Portia had seen just how unscrupulous William Finnegan really was. Putting the inmates into prostitution for profit wasn't much of a stretch of the imagination, especially considering the workhouse master apparently had no qualms about setting fire to his office to hide any evidence of his coverups.

"What was the name of the man again?" Portia asked as she rounded the edge of her desk.

A slow smile slid over Maisie's face, the fretful look in her eyes replaced with hope. "Arthur Strong."

Portia ripped a sheet of paper out of the top drawer of her desk and flipped back the lid on the inkwell. She scratched the name onto the paper, asking, "And what was the name of the place?"

"The River Maiden, I think," Maisie shrugged. "Though Sallie claims she was in a place called The Court before then." Portia dipped for more ink and scribbled the information down as Maisie asked, "Do you believe me?"

"I believe that you believe it," Portia said as she waved the paper, trying to dry the ink.

"But what are you going to do, miss?"

Portia thought about her options and then lifted her shoulders. "I'm not sure. I have a lot to think about."

"No one here will believe you, but I thought... Duncan says the guardians won't know about it. Although it might just be Sallie that this has happened to."

"I'll look into it."

Maisie's eyes went as wide as saucers. "You don't mean... You can't go in there, Miss Summerhill – you're a... people will talk!"

A wry smile touched Portia's lips. "You let me worry about that, Maisie."

"When is your next day off?"

Portia couldn't stop the deriding sound that slipped passed her lips. "Sorry, it's just that…" How could she word it so that the young woman wouldn't grow even more concerned about the goings on here? "My duties have kept me here for weeks on end."

A line appeared between Maisie's brows. "No day off?"

Portia shook her head as she folded up the piece of paper with the names on it. When she dropped it into her apron pocket, her fingers brushed the letter that she'd received that morning. Just thinking about the contents of that envelope made her heart skip a beat. Pressure was mounting from all sides, and she wondered just how much more she could take.

"I don't suppose having the fire in this place has helped, either."

Portia wrapped her arms around her middle, surprised at just how astute young Maisie Milne was. "No, it hasn't, but you mustn't concern your-self with such matters."

"You'll be safe, miss?"

"I will, Maisie," Portia said, though they both jumped when the door knocked loudly. Portia was halfway around the side of her desk when Matron Pursley opened the door.

"Miss Summerhill, I wondered if –" The matron's pugnacious gaze landed on Maisie and she scowled, sending the door wider as she stepped into the room. "What are you doing in here, Maisie Milne?"

Maisie opened her mouth, though Portia smoothly interrupted her, "I sent for her."

Matron's eyes swung between them both. "Why?"

"Because there is a national test that I want to put her name forward for."

"What on earth for?"

Portia bristled at the supercilious tone. "Because Maisie has the ability to be able to pass such a test."

Matron Pursley divided a narrow-eyed look between them both. "Is this true?"

Maisie nodded quickly, and the matron's mouth pinched white in discontent. "We shall see what the Master has to say about such a thing. Which reminds me," she pointed a thick finger in Maisie's direction. "Master Finnegan needs to speak to you."

"M-me? But w-why? I've done nothing wrong."

"Don't give me that – and don't you dare question me! You can wait in the hall," she spoke loudly over Maisie's protests, glowering at her as she scurried past. Matron closed the door firmly, confident in her command of the young woman that she would do as she was told. She inhaled sharply and peered at Portia. "You're getting too familiar with these charges," she informed her without preamble. "It's been noticed not just by me, either. Master Finnegan says that you're too soft – and I agree with him.

You fuss and cluck over them like a hen. It's not going to help any of these wretches in the end."

Portia didn't like the fact that her actions had brought Maisie under the attention of the workhouse master, but she held her tongue, allowing her dislike for the woman to show on her face. "I'm sorry that he feels that way. I am keen to see the children succeed, though."

Matron gestured at the door, "You have your favourites and it's not right."

Portia raised an apathetic shoulder. "As do you, Matron Pursley. As does every other member of staff under Master Finnegan's command."

The matron hadn't expected such a candid response and Portia took advantage of the momentary disconcertment. "But I'm sure Master Finnegan would enjoy the accolade that having the children of the workhouse attend – and even pass – national tests at the local school would bring him, don't you agree?"

Portia held the woman's glare for what felt like

an age before she huffed out of the room, slamming the door behind her for good measure. She considered following them, needing to know what they wanted with Maisie though she knew enough about the secrecy of this place to know that they wouldn't tell her.

Instead, she drew the letter and the piece of paper from her apron and considered her next move.

CHAPTER 18

*M*aisie was relieved to see two other girls, Emily and Clara, standing in the hall beyond the schoolroom door.

"What's going on?" she asked.

Emily shook her head and Clara replied, "Your guess is as good as mine!" Her thick London accent made her sound more aggressive, and Maisie hoped that Matron couldn't hear her through the sturdy wooden schoolroom door. "We was minding our own business when Matron called us out."

"To see the master, yes?"

"Yes, but why?"

Maisie tried to listen in at the door. She could make out voices but not what they were saying. She gnawed at her cheek, her nerves twitching and churning her guts. When Matron Pursley slammed out of the schoolroom, her face was thunderous, and the atmosphere charged with tension. Maisie glanced at Emily and Clara, wondering what could've transpired behind that closed door to tick off the old trout so much.

"Quickly now, don't dawdle," Matron Pursley's voice was sharp, echoing off the walls as she led them through a maze of dim corridors to a hall. She ushered the three girls into the room, issuing a rushed apology to the man sitting at the head of the polished table that dominated the room.

William Finnegan didn't look up. Several papers and a ledger were spread out on the polished surface before him. He dipped his pen into the open inkwell as if he was still sitting alone, unperturbed by the matron thrusting the three of them under his nose.

"Stand there," Matron nudged them into a line along the wall. "And close your mouth, Emily."

Maisie's eyes darted around the room. Several chairs were tucked up tightly to the table, and a plain wooden bench spanned the other wall, looking out of place in such a grand setting. The three girls exchanged glances, each uncertain of what to expect. After what seemed an age of waiting, the workhouse master set down his pen and eyed them, one at a time, drawing out the moment, causing Maisie's pulse to race.

"You are no longer children," he began without preamble. "As such, your roles within the work-house will change." His stern expression did nothing to soften the words as he told them how their duties would change. Her thoughts were else-where - with Sallie Bell. The stories about what had happened to the girl after she had been apprenticed out haunted her dreams. She briefly wondered if Matron had heard what she'd been talking to Miss Summerhill about. She risked a look at the matron who was nodding along to the master's intonation, though her attention snapped back to him when he added, "Of course, there will be no more time for your schooling."

Maisie couldn't help the gasp that slipped free, drawing a scathing look from him that sent shivers down her spine. A dark brow shot up in question and Maisie dropped her eyes to the floor, willing herself smaller.

Master Finnegan continued, "Because you are orphans, you will all be apprenticed out into service."

Maisie's head snapped up. "Do we have a choice, sir?" she blurted.

She felt the sharp sting of Matron Pursley's

hand against the back of her head before she even saw the woman move.

"Mind your place, girl," she hissed.

"Matron Pursley is right. There is no place here for impertinence."

"I'm sorry, Master Finnegan. This one is a bit big for her britches at times."

Displeasure rippled over his face, those intense dark eyes studying her. "What's your name, girl?"

Keep your nose clean.

Duncan's warning shimmered through her mind and for a moment, she considered lying but all that would do would result in a harsher punishment. She was already under the attention of the man who held her future in his palm.

"Maisie Milne."

"Ah, Miss Summerhill's star student," he drawled.

She watched as Finnegan and Matron Pursley exchanged a long, inscrutable look. Something passed between them, a silent agreement that Maisie couldn't decipher. But at that moment, she felt a dread settle in the pit of her stomach.

"Maisie, the workhouse has cared for you, fed you, kept you warm. Now, it's time for you to repay that kindness. You do that by doing as you're told and taking a job in service. The workhouse earns a small fee which will be used in some part to house and feed the other orphans you have grown up with. That's a fair exchange, wouldn't you say?"

Maisie clamped her mouth shut, angling her chin up at him in defiance.

Matron Pursley smacked her again. "Maisie, you ungrateful, insolent brat. You answer Master Finnegan this instant."

Maisie's thoughts were a whirlwind. The fear, the stories, the whispered warnings about girls who disappeared into the world, fighting for room. Her eyes filled with tears that she was determined not to let fall.

William Finnegan sighed, and he shook his head in irritation. "I don't have the time for this today. Which of you can write?"

Maisie and Emily timidly raised their hands. To Clara, he said, "Can you read?" She shook her head slowly. "Good. Make an 'X' here."

Curiosity overwhelming her fear, Maisie tried to catch a glimpse of the document that he held out to Clara. But Finnegan's watchful eye caught her movement. He tilted his head, a cunning gleam sliding into his narrowed eyes. "You're the one Miss Summerhill was speaking with—the girl from the yard the night of the fire, aren't you?"

"Yes, sir," Maisie whispered.

"The schoolmistress wants her to sit an exam, Mr Finnegan. A special test, she says."

William's eyes remained on Maisie's face for a moment, before they skimmed down to small form to her boots. "You can read and write?"

Her heart was pounding so loudly that she was sure the entire room could hear it. "Yes."

"You want to know what this document is?" His tone was mocking, and Maisie shook her head. "No, I didn't think so. Matron, you can take young Maisie in hand. I have something else in mind for her. Leave the other two here with me, will you?"

Just like that, Maisie knew that she had sealed her fate.

The protests of the other girls were drowned out by the roar in Maisie's ears as Matron Pursley dragged her from the room.

"Wait!" Maisie struggled against the biting grip around her arm. "Please, wait!"

But Matron was used to throwing around inmates bigger and much stronger than Maisie. She dragged her down the corridor. The cold, grey stone underfoot seemed to stretch endlessly, mirroring the bleak future that awaited her.

As she struggled, a chilling thought crossed her mind: the world outside the workhouse may be more terrifying than anything she had faced within its walls.

CHAPTER 19

*A*utumn had brought with it cold and damp air.

A thin layer of dried leaves was being whisked around the yard by brisk winds carrying a hint of rain. Cumulus clouds streaked across the pale blue sky as the sun made its final descent towards the horizon.

It felt odd to Maisie being out so late in the day. For as long as she could recall, her breaks had been taken mid-morning, followed by a short recess early in the afternoon, a time when mothers and children could unite. But now that she had joined the women's section, her entire routine had been upended.

The yard was much quieter without the joyous shouts and laughter of children playing with their wooden toys against the austere backdrop of the workhouse yard.

A few pairs walked about the enclosure in a leisurely manner, arms linked, almost as if they were taking a stroll through a town park. Maisie sat against one wall; her gaze drawn to other solitary figures scattered around the place. She'd heaved a sigh of relief when she'd emerged from the confines of the storage cupboard earlier that day and saw both Emily and Clara hard at work. They were still here. But there was little comfort to be drawn from not knowing what was going to happen next.

Three days with only one bowl of gruel and some tepid water a day had drained her to the point of exhaustion. Typically, after such punishing confinement, she would relish her time outside. But today, she could scarcely muster the energy to blink. During her time in the darkness, her mind had been consumed with thoughts of impending doom.

In her dreams, Sallie Bell wept, while William Finnegan cackled, black eyes blazing, as she was pulled toward a future that yawned like a gaping abyss before her. And even when she tried to awaken from the nightmares, she found herself still enveloped in the suffocating darkness. She'd left the cupboard and returned to work without complaint.

She split the rope, ignoring those who tried to draw her into conversation. She let the comments and looks slide off. Helpless fear dragged at her limbs.

When the hand clamped on her shoulder, she raised listless eyes. It took her a moment to focus on Miss Summerhill.

Concern creased the teacher's face. "Maisie – are you quite alright? I was calling you; didn't you hear me?"

Maisie looked around at the yard, unmoved.

"I've been worried about you. I tried to find you in between my lessons, but it's been difficult to get away," Portia waited a minute before she moved directly in front of Maisie, cutting off her view of the yard that had her so engrossed. She laid a hand against her forehead. "Maisie? Where have you been?"

"Storage room." Her voice felt rusty from lack of use, and she winced, swallowing to try and lubricate it.

"And these bruises on your arms? What are they from?"

Maisie lifted a shoulder. "Don't remember."

"Maisie…they moved you to the women's section."

Detached, she nodded. "No more school lessons."

"Maisie," Portia leaned down, eyes shining. "What happened to you when you left my schoolroom?"

Finally, Maisie met the teacher's tear-filled gaze. "I'll be leaving soon. I'll be like Sallie. I have no choice. I'm an orphan. No one wants an orphan."

"Did Matron tell you what happened to Sallie? Did she tell you where they took her for her to end up in such a place?"

"No, but I know people disappear from here all the time. I'll be one. So will Clara and Emily," Maisie heard the frantic knocking, but she held onto Miss Summerhill's gaze. "Master Finnegan said so. He made Clara sign something even though she couldn't read."

"What was it? You can read, so you should know."

"I couldn't see," Maisie replied. "I tried but… Master Finnegan knows. He knows all."

"You can't give up," Portia shook her shoulders. "I am trying to find out what is happening here. I believe you, Maisie. You have to stay strong; keep fighting."

"What's the point? That's my lot in life. A soiled dove but at least I'll have a roof over my head."

Portia clicked her tongue. "Where is the young

woman who sought me out to tell me what was going on here, the one with fire in her belly?" Miss Summerhill glanced over her shoulder and did a double take. She pointed up at the window to the men's dormitory where Duncan was banging on the glass. "Look, Maisie, *he* still wants you to fight."

He was still here.

In the darkness, when she'd been alone, she hadn't been able to find her way back to him. Yet, there he was, trying to gain her attention. As she met Duncan's inconsolable expression, she felt a little of the numbness wear off. Her feverish mind hadn't been able to work out which were dreams and which were reality. Clare, Emily, Duncan... They were all still here. She stepped away from the Miss Summerhill's concerned expression, lifting a hand up. In response, Duncan laid his hand against the glass.

"If you won't fight for yourself, do it for him, Maisie."

The schoolmistress' voice was tucked in low behind her, and Maisie found herself nodding. She could do it. Duncan had promised her that he would find his way back to her. Duncan was pulled away from the window and one of the other men filled the space, trying to find his mate. He'd had his turn.

Maisie spun back to Portia, filled with a

renewed energy. "I didn't see the document. The fact that Clara couldn't read seemed to please Master Finnegan. He had her sign it."

"The Master said he was pleased about the fact that she couldn't read?" Portia questioned.

"It was not so much the words he used but it was the smirk on his face," Maisie answered her after careful consideration.

"Who else was there with you?"

"Just Matron and us girls. No one else. He made Clara sign it and then I was taken by Matron and put in the cupboard, so I didn't hear anything more."

"Maisie…" The teacher cupped her face briefly and then moved her hands to her shoulders. "Please know that I am going to help you. I will do all in my power to find out what is going on here."

Maisie's heart skipped a beat and she blinked, not quite sure if she'd heard the other woman correctly. "You will?"

Portia nodded. "I won't let anything bad happen to you, okay?"

"What about Duncan?"

"I'm going to help you all."

The sudden hush over the yard drew their gazes toward the door. John Cobb stood at the threshold, scanning the yard. He spotted them and made his way over the stone yard. Maisie tucked herself back behind the teacher, her heart in her throat, although he seemed to be searching the square, his eyes swinging back and forth.

Portia waited until he was close enough that she didn't have to raise her voice. Maisie was impressed that the woman didn't seem to fear him. "Mr Cobb? Is everything alright?"

"You have a visitor?"

"A…what?"

"At the front door," he snapped. "Why else would I be out here skivvying for you?"

Maisie heard the soft exhale, though Miss Summerhill's tone was still mild. "Where is the visitor?"

"In my room," he retorted, though he wasn't looking at her. He was angling his head and Maisie realised that he was checking the inmates that passed by them. "Where else would they be?" Then he did look at her, and the annoyance in his face made Maisie shrink back more. "This is most irregular, Miss Summerhill. We don't offer a social meeting place in a workhouse for a reason."

"I'm afraid I have no control over what people choose to do of their own volition, thank you, Mr Cobb."

Maisie knew that such insubordination from an inmate would result in a beating, though he simply glared at her instead before he indicated the door with his head "This way."

Miss Summerhill offered her a reassuring pat on the shoulder and then trotted after the workhouse porter as he stomped back into the building.

PORTIA ALMOST COLLIDED with John Cobb as she stepped through the door. He was waiting in the narrow passageway.

"Have you seen her?"

Portia reared back, her mind stumbling as her heart raced in her chest. "Pardon?"

"Nellie Jones," he ground out impatiently. "Have you seen her?"

In the silence, Portia's nervous swallow made an audible click, and she shook her head quickly. "No, I'm afraid I haven't."

The porter speared his hands through his hair, making the tufts stand out from his head. Portia realised then that he was worried. After all the dreadful stories that she'd heard about him, the cruelty that she'd witnessed doled out by his hands, the fact that he seemed as frenzied as Duncan set off warnings in her head. He obviously cared for the pretty inmate a great deal. At that moment, she took pity on him.

She checked along the passageway behind him, ensuring it was clear before she quietly told him, "Matron oversees the women, as she is continuously reminding me. She locked Maisie Milne in the storage room after a meeting with Mr Finnegan. She was in there for almost three days. I don't know which one, but you might want to start by looking in those."

John Cobb bobbed his head once and then he was gone, his long legs crossing the yard towards the back gates that led to the outer yards. Portia hurried along the passageways, not hearing the echoes of the working day through the doors that she passed. Her mind was on her visitor. She let herself through several doors as she made her way into the belly of the building.

She darted into the porter's room, drawing up short when her puzzled frown smoothed out to one of shock as she met the startling green gaze staring back at her.

"Theo!"

"Hello, Lydia."

CHAPTER 20

"What are you doing here?" Portia's pleasure at seeing Theodore Whittonstall's handsome face quickly transformed into trepidation.

Theo regarded her as if the answer was self-evident. "To see you, of course. Why else?"

"How did you find me?"

"Your housekeeper gave me your forwarding address—after much persuasion. And a crown," he remarked with a hint of humour.

"You shouldn't have spent so much money," Portia murmured, warmth creeping up her neck. The cost of running the house in her absence was already significant, and she suspected Mrs Lazenby would be quite displeased about being put in such a position, especially since Portia had sworn the woman to secrecy. Portia surmised she might need to hire new staff once her business here was concluded.

"She claimed to have been forwarding my letters to you. Is that true?"

Portia regarded him for a moment. "Let's talk outside," she suggested, moving to the door, and holding it open for him. "The walls around here have ears if you know what I mean."

His expression was telling, but he obliged immediately, plucking up his hat from John Cobb's desk. He ushered her through the doorway so he could close it behind them. She'd almost forgotten what it was like to be in the presence of a gentleman, having grown too accustomed to the behaviours of John Cobb and William Finnegan.

Theo walked alongside her. In her periphery, she caught him taking a long, hard look at his surroundings. At the stunning array of autumnal colours on show in the thicket of trees that surrounded the workhouse. The workhouse itself, with its sandy-red façade. Walking alongside him was strange. Thankfully, he remained quiet until they reached the lane that ran perpendicular to the pathway. Checking that they were concealed enough by the hedgerow, she turned to him.

"What name did you use when you asked for me?"

Theo pursed his lips, his incisive eyes losing a little of their twinkle, and she could see that he was disappointed in that being her first question to him when she hadn't clapped eyes on him in months. That sensation niggled at her more than if he'd been cross with her.

"Portia Summerhill. Your housekeeper impressed upon me the importance of maintaining your alias, though for the life of me, I cannot figure out why. What is wrong with your real name?"

She wanted to blurt everything out to him, to finally offload the whole sorry story, but she was afraid that he would see her differently. "It's a long story, Theo. And this is neither the time, nor the place."

"Lydia... my darling, I hate to see you like this. And I'm not talking about your sad little outfit. You look exhausted. Please, let me take you home–"

"No." The word shot out, dropping like a stone between them, as she twisted away from his grip. The look of hurt was like a kick to her solar plexus. "Look, if you knew the real reason I was here..." She bit back the words. She wasn't that sure of him, obviously.

His green gaze roved her face, and she would hazard a guess that she looked a sight, compared to the way that he was used to seeing her. The silence stretched on between them, and she wondered if he was gauging how much damage would happen to his family's reputation by continuing their dalliance.

"You shouldn't be here. If someone connects you to the workhouse, then… well, I'm sure your mother would take to her bed for a year to recover."

His stance relaxed slightly, and she was happy to see that the twinkle of amusement was back. "There aren't enough smelling salts on God's green earth to counteract my mother knowing that her only son has today been inside a workhouse."

A reluctant laugh burst out of her mouth at the image of his uptight, snobbish mother lying in the frilly, frothy confine of her bed, bemoaning the fact that Lydia Foxhall had brought shame upon their house, just as she'd predicted would happen when Theo had started courting her.

"Goodness," she breathed. "That felt good."

"What did?"

"That's the first good laugh that I've had in ages."

His mouth hooked up on one corner in that lazy smile of his that made her heart flop about in her chest like a landed fish. "Then I would say that my work here is done."

"Thank goodness for you," she said, laying a hand on his arm.

His smile faded, and he was back to studying her closely. "You know, I thought you were mad when you said that you wanted to work. Madder still, when you took up training to become a teacher, considering teachers are never-married women."

She remembered the confusion and the quarrel that they'd had. It had been the first of many and she knew first-hand that poor old Mrs Whittonstall was despairing that her only son wouldn't give her up. She'd even called upon Portia at her home and demanded that she call it off with him. Stubborn to the core, Portia had refused to be the one to break her son's heart, even though there was a possibility that just by her embarking on this plan, she would ruin him. She couldn't give up the only man that she had ever loved. And he loved her.

But would he still do so once he knew her secret?

"Mother said that I should give you up, even then. That I needed to find a nice, uncomplicated soul to settle down and have children with," he said.

A hot knife of jealousy sliced her to the core. "Perhaps you should," she said, her voice thickened with emotion. "Perhaps she is right. I'm not being fair to you, Theo, not really."

He chuckled then, catching hold of her hands. That simple connection of his touch revived her, refilling up her reserves of determination that had been drained by the past few days. "I could no more give you up than a fish could give up water."

"Then it would just be a lizard, if you are to believe Charles Darwin and his cohorts."

Theo let rip a roar of laughter. Seeing him, so carefree, made her heart soar. She had missed him, more than she thought she would. And yet, she still had so much to do here. "Oh, my sweet girl, how I have missed you and your contrary wit. No wonder I love you so."

"Do you, Theo?"

He brought one of her hands to his mouth and kissed the backs of her fingers. "Yes, I really do – even after you vanished from your life, and mine, when I'd asked you to marry me."

"I left you a letter explaining that there was something I had to do before I could answer you." She remembered the joy of him proposing to her, and the nagging ache that there was still a part of her life that she needed answers to. "I wrote to you, too."

"Yes, you did, pretending that you were off galivanting around the country visiting friends, for what felt like an eternity. Then I hadn't heard from you in well over a month, Lydia. What was I supposed to think."

She'd been unable to write to him because she

hadn't been able to leave here. The housekeeper's letters to her had grown more urgent, telling her how his visits to her home had grown more frequent to demand answers on where she was. Mrs Lazenby had told her just how frantic with worry he was. Portia should have guessed that he would resort to bribery in the end. Poor Mrs Lazenby probably did it to have some peace from his pestering.

"You said that you'd wait for as long as it took for me to agree to marry you," she reminded him.

"And I meant it, though never in my wildest dreams did I think I'd have to trek halfway across the country to track you down – and in a work-house, no less!"

"I'm sorry, Theo. It's just something that I needed to do."

His brows crunched together, his gaze sliding to the building that was just visible through the trees. "You *needed* to come to the workhouse?"

She sighed, knowing how bizarre it must all seem to him. "Yes."

"Why?"

"Because I wanted to give back to the community?" Her flippant answer didn't amuse him.

"Lydia – Portia – whatever your blasted name is! Any other man would have walked away from you by now."

She pulled her hands away from him, wrapping them around her middle to try and comfort herself. She'd thought that she could handle losing Theo in all of this, that collateral damage was to be expected, but it still hurt her to hear it. "I know. In fact, you're probably better off distancing yourself before we go any further."

"But if you would just tell me what was going on here. Why you felt the need to disappear from your life…? I would understand."

Would he? Could he truly appreciate the driving need that had brought her to the doors of Brookford workhouse? She wasn't sure anyone could when she barely understood it herself. But, once the idea had taken root all those years ago, she knew that she couldn't accept being his wife until she had done what she'd set out to do.

"You should go," she told him. "Go far away from here. Find a girl that your mother would approve of, Theo. I couldn't bear to tarnish your life."

He growled in frustration, swept her up into his arms, and crushed her mouth with his. The kiss was fervent, demanding, aggravated…branding. "I can't," he muttered as he dragged his mouth from hers. "You're under my skin, Lydia. You annoy me to all damnation, but I cannot give you up. I love you. It's taken me a long time to find someone that

I want to spend the rest of my life with, and here you are.

Come with me now – leave this ludicrous place, with its sadness that's permeated the bricks, and that fearsome porter. Come home with me and begin our life together."

It sounded divine, and it would be so easy to give up all that she had worked for. To sink back into her comfortable world, with the silk dresses, maids and dinner parties. To wake up in a comfortable bed, with Theo by her side every day. The dream shattered when she thought of the pale faced inmates, fighting for survival behind the walls of the workhouse.

"Not yet," she replied. "I will come back, I promise. But for now, I must stay here and finish what I started."

"Very well," Theo said, though she could see that he didn't understand what drove her to be here in the first place. "But you will tell me what you're doing here when you come back?"

She nodded. "I will, though I'm not sure that your marriage proposal will stand once you know the truth."

"Then you don't know me half as well as I'd hoped," he quipped. He studied her as if trying to commit her features to memory. "You'll be safe here?"

"Yes," she said, and realised that lying came naturally to her now.

"Then I shall bid your goodbye but first… may I have one last kiss? To carry me over until the next time we meet?"

This time, when he took her in his arms, he was more like the Theo she remembered. The kiss was loving and sweet, and her heart still raced just as fast. Her fingers touched her mouth as he stepped back, trying to hold onto the memory of his touch. He quickly lifted his hat in farewell, and then he was strolling away along the lane towards a waiting carriage.

She made her way back along the pathway, letting herself in through the front door, even though Matron had forbidden it. She crossed the floor and opened the interior door, swallowing a scream when William Finnegan moved out of the shadows.

"Where have you been?"

Blood thundered in her ears, and her euphoria of seeing Theo evaporated as she was plunged straight back into this ugly world. "You scared me," she said, a hand against her chest.

He lounged against the wall. "You know you're not meant to use the front door, unless you're choosing to be an inmate here, too, Miss Summerhill."

His lazy drawl made her skin prickle with apprehension. "I know. There was a man at the door."

"Who?"

"Nobody special," she said a little too quickly. William folded his arms, and she rushed on. "An old acquaintance of mine who was…just passing through."

William stepped into the band of light afforded by the high-up window. "You forget that I can see everything from my quarters, Miss Summerhill. Everything," he emphasised the word in a harsh whisper. "I never kiss my old acquaintances in such a manner."

She refused to have her moment with Theo sullied by him. Annoyance licked through her. "If I had been allowed my allotted time off recently, Master Finnegan, I wouldn't have had to conduct my *private* business on a road."

He chuckled, unperturbed by her cheek. "This is what working for a living is about. Will we expect any more visits from your old acquaintance?"

"I highly doubt that."

"Perhaps it might be time to consider moving on, judging by the way your old acquaintance was touching you."

So, he'd been watching her for a while, intruding on a tender moment. She felt tainted by his tone of voice. His presence unnerved her, and she realised that he wanted to intimidate her. Only she wasn't an inmate. Her chin lifted in defiance, eyes glaring. He thrived on power, on being the owner of all he surveyed.

Her lips curved slightly as she murmured, "I will when I achieve all I set out to do by coming here."

CHAPTER 21

The news of Nellie Jones' disappearance had all the women in the dormitory on edge. If a woman favoured by the mighty John Cobb could vanish, what hope did any of them have?

Maisie tried her best to drown out the fearful chatter that filled the workrooms in the absence of Matron Pursley. She had believed Miss Summerhill when she said that she would try to help them. She took her usual perch on the bench nearest the window and waited for Duncan to emerge in the yard for his exercise. When she spotted his familiar form, she slipped down from her seat and hurried towards the door.

"Where do you think you're going?" Ethel Crabtree stepped into her path, her expression stern.

Maisie tried to sidestep her, hands on her hips, as she looked up at the older woman. "What's it to you, Ethel?"

"If you go out there, and they find you, you'll be done for. There's enough chaos happening in this place right now, Maisie, without you seeking out more trouble."

Murmurs of agreement echoed around the workshop, but Maisie held her ground. "I need to see Duncan."

Ethel's sigh conveyed her frustration, but she stepped aside, remarking, "On your head be it."

Gratefully, Maisie pulled on the door, stepped into the yard, and made a beeline for Duncan. She caught his hand and pulled him away from the others.

"What's the matter?" Duncan looked about the yard, rattled by her behaviour.

"My days are numbered," she told him. "Finnegan pulled me and two others into his office. He had one of them sign a form and said that we were being apprenticed out."

His eyes popped wide. "When?"

"I don't know," she said quickly, "but I told Miss Summerhill. She said that she's going to do her best to help."

He dragged a hand down his face. "Can you

trust her, Maisie? Not one of the staff here has a good bone in their bodies!"

"She's different," she stated, hurt that he would question the loyalty of the schoolmistress. "There's something about her that is very different from the others."

"I don't like it."

"What choice do we have, though? I wanted to warn you. When it took you a while to come out, my heart almost… I could have wept when I saw that you were still here."

"They haven't gotten rid of me yet," he said, then he framed her face in his big hands, his mouth curving at the edges. He rested his forehead against hers. She laid hers over his, eyes closing as unshed tears stung the backs of her eyes. "I hate that I can't help you. Nellie Jones has gone."

"I know," she murmured. "It's got everyone on edge. If she isn't safe, then none of us have a chance."

"We have to get word to someone, let them know that people are vanishing."

"Miss Summerhill –"

He shook his head. "Someone other than staff, Maisie. The men have said that the next one of us who can afford to leave, to find some work, will tell the police. They're worried about their wives."

"It's never the married women, so their fears are

unfounded. Only single mothers and orphans, Duncan. People that no one will miss. I'll ask Miss Summerhill. She can go for us. I'm sure that I can convince her to help."

"You must be careful," he told her, his eyes shining. He leaned his head down and her breath caught in her throat. "I can't bear the thought of losing you."

She pressed onto her tiptoes and her lips met his in a moment of stolen bliss. Sensations crashed over her; the warmth of his mouth against hers, their breaths mingling. Her heart soared with the feeling of being in his arms. Joy burst inside, filling her with love when he kissed her back. For that moment, all that existed was them. His arms came around her, securing her to him as the kiss deepened.

Their embrace was suddenly shattered when Matron Pursley appeared out of nowhere. With a swift, brutal motion, she grabbed Maisie by the collar of her worn dress and yanked her away from Duncan, bellowing for help. Maisie was thrown unceremoniously onto the hard ground, even as Duncan tried to reach for her.

Pain chased her breath from her body and Matron Pursley's twisted expression filled Maisie's vision.

"You filthy trollop!" she spat, and brought the cane down onto Maisie's prone form.

"No!" Duncan yelled, lunging forward to yank the cane from the matron's grip before she could bring it down on Maisie a second time. "Don't you dare lay a hand on her!"

The matron's eyes narrowed to slits of fury. "I dare very much, boy. Give that back to me."

Duncan held it aloft, his eyes not leaving hers. "Maisie, get up now."

"Stop it! Please, Duncan, before it's too late—"

Maisie did as she was told, scrambling to her feet, her blood running cold when the foreboding figures of the workhouse Master and John Cobb appeared in the yard, drawn by the commotion.

"Burke, you bloody idiot!" John Cobb hissed, moving quickly to restrain the young man. Duncan struggled against him, but John's grip was like iron.

Duncan dropped the cane, his eyes not leaving Maisie's as his struggling form was pulled away from her by the porter and Finnegan.

"Duncan!" Maisie sobbed, scrambling to her feet, and reaching out towards him before he disappeared into the bowels of the building, still writhing, and yelling her name.

A sharp pain erupted on Maisie's cheek as Matron Pursley backhanded her, knocking her back to the ground. "That's enough out of you," she bellowed, pointing at her with the recovered cane. "You'll get no supper, and you'll be joining the mad imbeciles in the refractory ward."

As she lay there on the cold ground, the sound of Duncan's struggles fading away, Maisie felt a sinking despair engulf her.

What had she done?

CHAPTER 22

Maisie was shoved into the dormitory.

The door slammed shut behind her, and she heard the distinctive grinding sound of the lock turning. For a moment, she wanted to pound her fist against the door and demand answers. But she knew that it would be futile. Matron Pursley had threatened her with a longer time in the refractory ward if she refused to cooperate.

She'd already spent a night in there. Listening to the howls of raving lunatics in the ward felt like a thousand needles pricking her already tortured mind.

So, she'd remained silent, allowing the matron to drag her up the stairs and into the dormitory. She'd listened to the insults and rage of Mrs Pursley. About how orphans like her were the scourge of society and that one day, she would learn just how little she mattered in this world.

Slowly, she turned and faced the room. A sea of pale faces stared back at her, silently watching. She walked to the centre of the room, past the line of iron bed frames packed closely together on either side of the room.

She slipped off her boots and tucked them under the foot of the bed before climbing onto her thin mattress. Pulling the threadbare woollen blanket over her feet, she angrily wiped at the tears streaking her face.

It was Ethel Crabtree who broke the silence first. "I told you what would happen."

"Why do you do it, Maisie Milne?" Doris Gray chimed in. "It's always you."

"That's enough," Maggie Sutton muttered, rising from her bed. "Are you alright, Maisie?"

Maisie sniffed and nodded, knuckling away the tears.

"Was it the storage cupboard this time?"

"Refractory ward," Maisie replied softly.

"Overnight?" Doris Gray asked, her tone filled with horror at the thought. A shudder rippled around the room as Maisie nodded again.

Maggie sighed, and Maisie's bed dipped as the older woman joined her. "You don't help yourself.

Orphans like you must keep their heads down and mouths shut. You know this."

Maisie sniffed. She'd spent most of last night with her hands pressed against her ears to close off the moans and bloodcurdling screams of the mad who'd raved and howled at the night sky.

"Aren't you going to tell her about Duncan?" Martha asked.

Maisie looked up sharply, her gaze moving from Martha to the pained expression on Maggie's face. "Tell me what?"

Maggie stared at Martha, scowling. "Hasn't the girl been through enough?"

Fear made Maisie's mouth dry. "What's happened to him?" But she knew. As her blood froze in her veins, she could tell by the looks exchanged around the dormitory that it wasn't good news. "Please... tell me."

Maggie sighed, avoiding Maisie's eyes. Her mouth compressed "We've had word from the men's day room that he's gone. But nothing's confirmed. He might be in a storage room, just like you've been."

Maisie stared at them all. They knew as well as she did that Mr Finnegan didn't punish the men in the same way as Matron did. His was public humiliation, just as John Cobb had done to poor young Edmund.

Maisie shook her head, her mind reeling, unable to comprehend the words settling in her heart. She needed to know, to see him, to touch him.

"Where is he?" Maisie tried to pull away from Maggie, but Maggie held her tight.

"He's disappeared," Maggie murmured. "No one's seen him since he was dragged off the yard yesterday."

CHAPTER 23

*T*he candle flame guttered and danced, drawing her eye back from staring through her bedroom window at the black of night, where the moon crescent flirted with the clouds.

Sleep had eluded her for hours until she'd finally given up. She'd then propped herself up in bed, trying to lose herself in a book, which usually helped on nights like this one, but at some point, her turbulent thoughts had crowded out the words.

Theo's visit had shaken her. Seeing him had reminded her that life – his life –had continued without her in it. How the world had simply carried on troubled her, reminding her that she'd come here with a specific task in mind, and yet she was no closer to her end goal. She felt as if she'd been wasting her time here, beating at the immovable barriers of mystery that surrounded this place.

Now, that thought, coupled with the knowledge that she knew things were amiss here and how powerless she was to stop any of it haunted her. In the dark corners of her mind, part of her wanted to give up. Theo claimed he would wait for her, but a man's patience only went so far.

She pushed back the bed covers now, as the candle flame hissed, warning her that she didn't have long before the flame ran out of wick. She shook her head with impatience after she'd opened the small door to her cupboard. In the upheaval of the past few days, it had slipped her mind to collect some spare candles. She'd have to go downstairs and get one. Trepidation hummed along her veins. She felt safe behind the locked door of her bed chamber, but these days, it was always dark when she readied herself for her working day. She would need some light to be able to wash and dress in the morning.

She stood before her bedroom door, her hand hesitating above the brass handle. The coolness of the night sent a shiver up her spine, and a fox screaming in the woods beyond the yard prickled the hairs on the back of her neck.

Taking a deep breath, she gripped the handle

and turned it, wincing as the door creaked open like a sigh. She paused at the top of the stairs, listening for any signs of life. The passageway ahead was dark. The silence was palpable, save for the whisper of the wind outside and the distant, haunting hoot of an owl.

Holding the hem of her gown, she began her descent, each step releasing an agonising groan from the old wooden staircase. As she moved, the shadows grew longer. The walls seemed to lean in to whisper their secrets to her, and an inexplicable feeling of being watched crept over her.

Halfway down, she froze. Was that a shadow flickering at the bottom of the staircase? Or merely her imagination, conjured from the blend of darkness and fear? Was it the wind? Rumours that the ghosts of the past still roamed these hallways taunted her mind.

The candle she held cast a trembling circle of light. She strained her ears and heard what sounded like a distant, muffled sob. It seemed to come from nowhere and everywhere, seeping from the very bricks that surrounded her. Dread thickened the air, tainted with secrets, making it hard to breathe. She hesitated, scanning the darkness behind her that pulsated with unseen dangers.

The sharp sting of hot wax that ran over the

backs of her fingers from the candle she held kicked her inert mind into action and she began downwards once more. Standing here alone was scary enough – standing here in enforced darkness just wasn't acceptable.

Finally, she reached the ground floor. The labyrinthine corridors of the workhouse stretched out ahead. She held the candle aloft. The scullery was just at the end of the corridor – a path she'd walked many, many times in the daylight. It wasn't too far to go.

Drawing a deep, steadying breath, Portia ventured forward, holding an image of the cuddy in her mind as the weight of the workhouse's oppressive history pressed in around her. The oil lamps had been turned down low, casting a gauzy glow that barely penetrated the gloom of the dimly lit corridor. The instinct to go back up to safety warred within. Her breath escaped in bursts, and she ran the last few steps to reach the door. She fell in through the door, holding the candle aloft and squinting through the gloom to see what she was doing. She added three candles to her pocket and was on her way back along the corridor when she heard it again – a sob.

This time, it was closer, more distinct. More pain-filled.

She wheeled, sending the light in her hands crazy as she checked all around her. A dull thud and a cough drew her attention to the kitchen. As she hesitated, contemplating whether to go forward or to flee back to the protection of her room, she felt it—a cold draft, as if someone had just passed by her. At that moment, she knew she was not alone.

A cough again, and a long moan.

She tiptoed to the edge of the archway that opened into the area where food was prepared for the inmates. Moonlight spilt into the room, casting elongated, eerie shadows that seemed to come alive with every flicker of the curtains. A shadow twisted quickly, hands rising into a defensive position when her candlelight melded with the moonlight to illuminate the room. The action caused another groan and the shadow morphed into a man who leaned on the table, holding his side, his face hidden behind long tendrils of dark hair.

"Mr Cobb?"

"Go away." The sound was guttural and raw. Even in the light, she saw something drip off his face and splash onto the table.

She lifted the candle higher, as he shuffled awkwardly from her light. "What's –"

"Did you hear me?" He snarled, his head snapping up, revealing a bloody, torn face. "Get out of here!"

Portia recoiled, a hand cupping the scream as she stared in horror at the ravaged face. She stared. "W-who did that to you? Was it an inmate?"

"No."

"I'll go fetch Matron," she turned but his hoarse cry stopped her, and she looked back.

"No...one... Fetch no one," he panted, dragging a sleeve across his mouth. He spat his mouthful of blood onto the floor. "Just go."

"I can't leave you here, John. You're going to bleed to death."

"Probably," he coughed.

John wilted as if the action had drained what little life remained in him. Slowly, he folded to the floor, sliding to the ground like a ragdoll. He landed against the table, his legs splaying out, as he gasped.

Portia grabbed the extra candle out of her pocket and lit it, adding a puddle of wax to the table before she jammed it in to stand there. The additional light edged back the darkness, alleviating her fear of the dark. She worried that whoever had done this was still lurking.

"Who did this to you?"

His ragged breathing punctured the air as she

searched for a bowl and filled it from a bucket under the sink.

"Let me alone, blasted woman," he groused as she crouched in front of him.

Ignoring his mutterings, she dunked a cloth in the bowl and dabbed it to his face. "You need a doctor, John. You're going to need stitches."

His hand came up to push her away, but he could only lift it partially off the floor before it dropped back down. She worked quickly, offering him some water when he asked for it.

His head fell back. His one eye had swollen shut; his eyebrow split open. The other eye rolled back as if he was trying to hold onto consciousness. He mumbled something and Portia paused in her ministering. "Say that again?"

"Not worth saving," he whispered. He pushed feebly at her and then his hand slumped, jangling his pocket as it landed on his leg. Struck by a thought, Portia slipped her hand into his pocket and found his keys.

She unhooked them from his belt and bounced them on her palm. She studied his face, gnawing on her lip.

He'd warned her to leave him alone. Whatever had happened here couldn't be good. But, as much as she despised him, she couldn't leave him like this. She swapped the candle on her plate for a fresh one and then spotted a lamp lying on its side on the floor in the corner. Perhaps he'd brought it in here.

She lit that instead and headed for the infirmary ward.

CHAPTER 24

*M*aisie's eyes flew open as soon as the lock slid back. Maybe it was years of living in a workhouse that made her a light sleeper, borne out of a strong survival instinct. She lay still for a moment, holding her breath in the darkness as she listened to the footfall on the floorboards. Too light for Matron. Too quiet – the woman didn't care if she disturbed the inmates or not. A soft circle of light paused by several beds, and Maisie heard the rustling and whispers. When she lifted her head, she saw Miss Summerhill holding a gas lamp aloft, peering into the beds as if checking the bodies that huddled within them.

"Maisie? Are you in here?" She called out, and the whispering in the room grew louder.

"Here," Maisie rolled up into a sitting position.

Miss Summerhill beckoned her closer. Maisie sat up, slipping her boots on. Maisie followed the woman to the door, listening as she assured the other inmates that all was well and that they should go back to sleep. Though Maisie knew that this unusual activity would unnerve them all and that none of them would sleep.

"What's going on?"

Miss Summerhill hushed her, laying a finger against her lips and then pointing along the corridor, indicating that Maisie goes first. Through door after door they went, moving quickly but quietly and Maisie was amazed that the teacher couldn't hear her heartbeat thundering as she followed her. Out through the back door and across the yard. Maisie risked a look back at the workhouse, wondering if she was right to trust the other woman at all. They stepped through the gateway in the yard wall and walked across the gravel toward the infirmary.

"Where are we going?" Maisie asked, a little louder now that there was some distance between them and the workhouse. "Miss Summerhill?"

"I'll explain all in a moment, Maisie," Portia replied. She opened the door and held it back for Maisie, though the young girl hesitated. "I need your help, Maisie. Agatha asked for you specifically."

As if on cue, the nurse poked her head through the interior door. "This is a job for a doctor, you know. Not me, and certainly not her."

Miss Summerhill looked vexed at the comment. "We must patch him up for now, Agatha. I will send for Doctor Jenkins at first light when I can be sure that he will survive."

Maisie hovered at the threshold. "What is going on?"

Agatha pushed the door open and shook her head gravely. "See for yourself."

Maisie stepped into the long room. The tang of metal and medicine made her nose wrinkle. Several lumps filled the beds, though there was only one light illuminating the room. Maisie held her breath, though even after just a few steps, she knew that it wasn't Duncan there. She drew up short when she recognised just who it was. Uneasily, she looked back at the two women.

"Who did that to him? Was it Duncan?"

Portia waved a hand. "No time for questions. Agatha said that we could count on you not to breathe a word about what you see here."

"A-alright," Maisie stammered. "Though I'm not sure that I want to help him."

Agatha snorted in agreement. Portia tutted at them both, crossing to the bed. "He's badly hurt." She set down the lamp on the side.

Maisie saw the arrangement of a needle and thread, alongside torn-up rags and a brown glass bottle laid out on a table next to him.

"Maisie, you hand me what I need."

"Me?"

Agatha held up her hands and retreated several steps. "I am not getting involved in whatever this is. I've shown you where the things you need are, but I am not risking what happened to Nellie Jones, happening to me. You're on your own." With that, the nurse retreated through a door at the other end of the ward.

In the ensuing silence, Maisie could tell that Miss Summerhill didn't care much for the refusal, and she met the schoolmistress' implored look. She sighed and crossed to the bedside. "What do you need?"

They worked together speedily, cleaning the wounds on the porter's face. Maisie held out bandages and clean rags, watching as Miss Summerhill clumsily attempted to stitch the skin in two places. John Cobb moaned more than once, though just as they were finishing, his left eye sprang open. Maisie recoiled as if facing a cobra.

"Easy, Mr Cobb," Portia began.

His eyes wheeled about the ward. "How did I get in here?"

"Nurse Agatha and I managed between the two of us. Maisie is here and is helping you, too."

His breath hissed between clenched teeth when she dabbed at the corner of his mouth that had started to bleed again. "I thought I told you to leave me be."

"Well, I wasn't going to leave you there, Mr Cobb. I'm sorry, but I wouldn't leave a wounded animal, even if it was trying to bite me."

Maisie tried to gauge the porter's reaction. She gnawed at her lip. She really ought to be seen and not heard at this very moment, but she couldn't hold the question in any longer. "Where's Duncan?"

Both of them looked at her, though Maisie was only interested in the porter's reaction.

His head lowered. "I don't know."

Maisie's fists clenched and she stepped closer to his bed. "Yes, you do! What did you do to him for him to beat you like this?"

He snorted derisively then, his one eye conveying how ridiculous he thought her to be. "He didn't do this to me."

"Who did then?" Portia countered; her hand paused in its dabbing.

John Cobb considered her a moment and then looked back at Maisie. "I don't know what happened to him, miss."

Miss Summerhill grew sterner with him. "John,

what is going on here? With all of these people vanishing?"

His mouth compressed and he scratched a thumbnail against the linen sheets covering his legs. "You shouldn't have brought me here."

"Then let me fetch the doctor?" Portia offered. "Please. This all needs proper attention. You're going to get an infection...you might even lose an eye, Mr Cobb." He paused for a moment and then reluctantly nodded. Portia turned to Maisie. "Go to my schoolroom. Get me paper and ink. There's an envelope in the middle drawer. Fetch it here. Here, take these keys. Can you do that?"

"You cannot give an inmate some keys," he snapped. "Have you lost all your senses?"

Portia tsked. "You're in no position to lecture me, Mr Cobb. Besides, whilst I wait for Maisie to fetch me what I need, you and I are going to have a little chat." She glanced at Maise and nodded encouragingly. "I'm trusting you, Maisie. I'm going to get to the bottom of where Duncan is."

Maisie nodded and darted through the door, keys in hand. She had to trust the teacher, too.

"You're a fool," John Cobb's voice was low, his laugh more of an exhale of breath. "She'll be out of the door and gone. She won't come back."

"Oh, ye of little faith." Portia set the bloodied rags on the side, dipped her hands in the bucket to rinse them and then perched at the edge of his bed as she dried her hands on her dirty apron. "Now, why don't we use this time to answer some of my questions?"

His head came off the pillow once more, his good eye open and wary. "It's no good. You can't stop it. You can't stop him. No one can."

"Stop who?" Portia leaned closer when he didn't reply. Thirst for answers pushed her on. "Who did this to you? Was it William Finnegan?" He studied her in the soft light, roving her face. His nod was slight.

Her brow furrowed. "Why did he?"

"I'll tell you all you want to know," he said, his words distorted out of the one side of his mouth. Just the action of speaking was causing him pain. "But first I have a question for you."

"Very well."

"Where do I know you from?"

She swallowed then and it was her turn to fidget. She straightened the filthy apron covering her thighs and brushed a stray hair off her face with the backs of her fingers, a small smile edging up the corners of her mouth. Her sigh was soft, accepting.

It was time.

She tilted her head as she looked at him. "Because we have, Mr Cobb. Many, many moons ago."

The air was still, pregnant, as he stared at her.

"I was an inmate here."

CHAPTER 25

"I knew it," his head dropped back against the pillow, his breath leaving his body in a deep sigh and his eyes closed. "I knew I'd seen you before."

He was so still that, for a moment, she thought he'd lost consciousness again. Panicked that she wasn't going to get the answers she so desperately needed, she gave him a shake, "Mr Cobb?"

"I'm still here," he groused. "More's the pity."

"I answered your question. Now, tell me why William Finnegan did this to you."

He stared at the ceiling. "I started it."

"Started what?"

"The fight."

Portia frowned. "I thought you were both fast friends."

John Cobb's mirthless laugh rattled in his chest. "No. Far from it. But we are bound by secrets and greed, Miss Summerhill."

A cold sweat broke out on her skin as disquiet prickled her body. "To do with the people who vanish from here."

It wasn't a question, but John nodded anyway. "Yes."

"Where do they go, Mr Cobb?"

He blinked, meeting her gaze fleetingly and then looking at the space above him. "They go wherever will pay us the most."

"What does that mean?" she asked, clutching his arm. "Where are you sending them all? Into prostitution?"

He hesitated. Frustrated, she gripped what was left of his shirt. "John, these are people. With hopes and dreams. They have families and loved ones who need to know what has happened to them—"

"No, they don't. They're the ones who won't be missed. People whose bodies aren't claimed after they die here. Some...people don't even know that they've arrived here."

Portia's heart jolted. *People like Elsie and Thomas... like her mother....*

John carried on, "Parishes don't want the additional cost and burden of burying them, though sometimes they don't know that they're burying empty caskets."

Her heart thumped in her chest. "Empty...? Where are the bodies, John?"

A cynical smile twisted his mouth. "We've sold them. Medical students. They buy corpses for doctors to practice on, I presume."

"Like a resurrectionist?"

John's brow moved a little, acerbic light gleaming in his one open eye. "Of course not. That's illegal. The law changed in 1844 banning workhouse officials from profiting from the sale of corpses," he turned his head to impress on her his next words. "But the fact remains that the demand for cadavers is still there. Surgeons and hospitals are crying out for corpses as the knowledge of surgery grows. It used to be just convicted criminals who'd been hung, and pauper's bodies who weren't claimed forty-eights after death. But you've been in the deadhouse here, Portia. How many bodies are in there at any one time?"

She recalled the room – bare brick and coffins collected together, with shrouded bodies, all awaiting collection.

"Once that coffin is shut, they don't know what they're burying, do they? What's in there?"

His shoulder moved in part shrug, part annoyance. "Sometimes dissected body parts that the hospital can't explain away. Sometimes, they just contain rocks. When we first started to see the money that could be made, well it was more than I was making in a quarter of a year. Just from one body that no one wanted anyway."

Portia stared at him, aghast. "That was a person, John. Full of hopes and dreams!"

"They were dead – they could hardly give their opinion. And the beauty of it is because a corpse cannot legally belong to anyone, we weren't doing anything illegal."

"So, you were skating in the grey area of the law?"

He nodded. "And making a good income from it. I was happy with the extra money, and no one missed the dead. Then things started to change."

Portia waited, knowing that she wasn't going to like what was to come, but needing to know anyway.

"Doctors complained that the bodies that once came from the hangman's noose were superior quality. This was generally because they were well-fed and younger. Students could better understand the anatomy of these corpses. Poorhouses were filled with old, worn-out people at the end of their lives.

When we realised that the surgeons paid more for the younger, healthier cadavers that hadn't been ravaged by age or disease, Billy came up with a way to meet that more lucrative demand."

Warily, she said, "You murdered people."

He broke the look, resuming his stare at the ceiling once more. "They don't want people with outward signs of being killed – at least, we didn't want to raise suspicion on how we were coming by these people. Billy, he… it was his idea."

"What was?"

"Do you know what carbonic oxide is?"

She shook her head.

"It's a gas produced by coal when it's burned. It's poisonous, Portia. If you breathe it in for long enough, it will kill you."

A conversation bloomed in her mind, of something the reverend had said at the meeting she'd attended. "Finnegan studied chemistry, didn't he?"

John nodded. "That he did. As he constantly likes to remind me. He came up with the idea. A coal fire, Portia. He built a stove for it. There's a chamber, with a series of pipes connecting to it. It captures the gas.

All that needs to be done is to light the coal fire in the stove. There's a room behind the porter's room. It connects to a cellar underground where the pipes feed into it…"

A partition in the wall revealed a small narrow door, hidden mostly by a bookshelf. Low down in the corner of the wall... Portia sucked in a breath as memories crashed into her mind. She glared at him through tear-filled eyes. "Go on."

"At first, the people in there would shout and cry out. The downside to choosing healthier people is that they are stronger. They would fight back. Some would claw at the door and cling to the opening high up in the wall that we opened to let the gases out afterwards. Billy then said that I had to give them something to drink to make them sleep. It would have laudanum or something similar in it."

Her eyes closed, spilling her tears down her cheeks. She remembered it all. The tea that he brewed for her. The baby crying. She could remember it all now, so painfully clear.

"My mother..."

For the first time, she saw something akin to regret in his face. "For what it's worth, I wanted to choose indoor relief for her, for you both. She was a very beautiful woman. You look a lot like her. Same eyes..." He lifted a hand to her face, but she recoiled.

"You killed her. You killed my mother and brother."

He didn't react to the vehemence quivering in her voice. "I didn't kill any of them. I gave them the drink and put them in the cell. The gas did the rest.

Not a mark on them, other than the ones who turned bright red."

"Semantics, Mr Cobb."

"The way I see it, all we've done is supplied a demand, all in the name of scientific progress."

Portia leaned back, her mind reeling with astonishment that he seemed so blasé about this. "Who lit the fire to make the gas?"

"Sometimes me, sometimes him."

He'd said it so casually. Disgusted, she said, "You're murderers, Mr Cobb. Both of you."

He coughed, the sound causing him to groan. He dragged the back of his hand across his mouth, wiping at the bloody spittle there. "Doesn't matter now, does it? I'm done for."

"Why didn't you kill me, too? What was special about my mother and my brother?"

He shifted in the bed, a hand at his ribs. He panted as though waiting for the pain to subside. "There was something different about your mother. She was defiant, right to the end. Your father had died in a shipwreck, she told me. She was going to Southampton to meet his captain. She had no other family, she said.

"I tried to stop Billy. I asked him to let this one go. Just one, I said. It was the first time I'd defied him and he...

I am not allowed to have favourites, you see. He

said that he would see to it that I was hung for everything that I'd done. He'd set everything up to look like I was the one who'd orchestrated it all. My father was a blacksmith. I know about metal, and about making iron pipes."

Portia relaxed her hands where she'd gathered into her tightly balled fists, infuriated by his selfish melancholy. She wiped at her eyes. He could only see how *he'd* been the victim affected by it all. She brought him back to the subject. "But my mother did have a family, Mr Cobb. My father had a sister."

More blood came up as he coughed. This time, she handed him a rag to wipe his mouth. "Yes. You were collected up by a policeman and whisked away. Questions were asked and we showed them entries into the records. It had taken a while for you to be collected, by which time your mother's body was already gone. Billy had to dance the verbal polka to get us out of that one. I don't know how he explained it away, but he did. We had to be more careful after that."

"Entries not being made," she guessed, and he inclined his head. "How could they be here if there's no trace of them being here in the first place?"

"We'd take in waifs and strays, then must wait to see if anyone came calling. A delicate balancing game, orchestrated by Finnegan."

"And nothing to do with you?"

He watched her, something dark and ugly moving in his façade. "I told you I tried to stop him, Miss Summerhill. More than once. Every time I defied him, I was punished, just like an inmate. He would take it out on those I cared about."

Portia's brows met when she heard the pain in his tone. "Women like Nellie?"

He nodded then, picking at a hang nail, his voice flat. "Nellie was different. She didn't care that I had this reputation. I think she liked it. She made me laugh the night she got here. It had been a long time since I'd laughed. After his wife died, William's attention was elsewhere.

The undertaker would turn up to collect the bodies and I'd have extra bodies that Finnegan didn't know about. I'd switch up the coffins, and then pocket the extra funds. I was hoping to save up enough money to leave this job, to just disappear with Nellie and get away from Finnegan.

I don't know how he found out about it, maybe one of the collectors told him. Billy said that he'd had to sell Nellie's body in lieu of monies I stole from him."

She covered her mouth to conceal her gasp. "Her and the boy?"

"The boy would have been sold to a childless family. That's how he usually worked," his eye rolled as he seemed to fight for a breath. "At least, I didn't see the boy's body when he showed me Nellie. That's when I snapped." He lifted his hands and Portia noted the broken skin along his knuckles. "I tried to fight him, for Nellie. For the others that I loved…"

She blinked, her mind racing. "My brother? Was he one of the ones sold?"

"The infant was dead in the morning," John muttered, eyes closing as his hands flopped to the bed. His breath seesawed in and out of his body. "He was sick that night you arrived. You said… you remembered…"

"I remember small parts of it. You, the porter's office… I was only young."

"You have her eyes. I knew that we'd met before…"

They were silent, each lost in thought. Portia had wanted to know what had happened to her mother. She knew the truth, but it didn't bring her any comfort. Her mother's body had been sold like property. Dissected and buried in a random grave. She didn't even have the comfort of being able to visit the grave.

"Why are you telling me all this now? You know that I can't keep this to myself. I must go to the police, John. This has to end."

His laugh rumbled around his chest like stones

in a bucket. "Go ahead. He has everything covered up. Others have tried to stop him and failed. You don't think that others don't know? He pays them off. Ten pounds a body, Portia. That's more than some make in half a year. And we've been moving many bodies to the hospitals. Here, in the country, where no one looks at it too closely because there aren't the funds, we can get away with it. Even if you did have proof, the fire destroyed the records."

"You could tell people, John. The same as you're telling me now."

His lips moved upwards though she couldn't tell if it was a smile or a snarl. "You think I'll avoid the noose, Portia?"

She stood then, furious. Even when his body was broken, he still wasn't prepared to face up to the crimes he'd committed. She straightened her dress, pushed the table back a little and collected up her lamp.

"My name isn't Portia. You might not have the strength to end this, but I do. That's why I came here."

CHAPTER 26

The damp morning air enveloped her as she left the infirmary ward. Clutching the edges of her shawl closer, her breath misted in front of her. As she crossed the gravel driveway, her steps were faintly illuminated by the light from her lamp. The looming dawn painted the sky with shades of pale blue and lavender, the blackness of the trees emerging from the darkness. Her scattered thoughts began to coalesce into a plan. She wondered about the time. She needed to contact both the guardians and the local constabulary. She deliberated on which evidence to gather first before departing to plead for swift action against the horrors within these workhouse walls.

But first, she needed to find Maisie.

She tried to estimate the time that had passed

while she spoke with John Cobb. Portia hastened along the darkened passageways, her eyes adjusting to the gloom just enough to make out familiar surroundings. Upon reaching her schoolroom, her heart sank. The door stood ajar. There was no sign of Maisie.

The door creaked softly as she peered around its edge, the weak light from her lamp spilling inside, to make sure she wasn't hidden under the desk.

"Maisie?" she whispered, her voice faintly echoing in the empty space. The room seemed to swallow her call, offering back stifling silence.

A rush of anxiety overtook Portia. She retraced her steps to the hallway, her voice rising with desperation, "Maisie!"

The long corridor absorbed her calls, echoing back only the muffled sound of her own voice. A knot of worry tightened in her gut. Every nerve screamed a warning, aware that William Finnegan lurked nearby. Terrifying scenarios clouded her mind, each more dreadful than the last.

Tentatively, Portia began edging along the walls leading to the dormitories. When frightened, an animal would return to where it felt safe. Maisie would surely feel safer amongst those she lived with. With each step, a niggling doubt grew stronger inside. Was John Cobb correct? Had

Maisie stolen the keys and fled this place in search of Duncan?

Upon reaching the heart of the sprawling building, Portia paused, ears straining for any sign of movement. Just as the thought of William Finnegan ominously loomed in her mind, the man himself emerged from the shadows. His eyes, alight with madness, caught the dim light, revealing a twisted grin that could curdle blood.

"Miss Summerhill, wandering outside your quarters at such an ungodly hour," his voice dripped with malevolent sweetness. "To what do we owe this pleasure?"

Portia steeled herself as he took a step further into the light. Panic pooled in the pit of her stomach when the knife in his hand glinted, and she saw the terror mirrored in Maisie's eyes. He had the young woman gripped to him, his other hand over her mouth, though his attention remained on Portia. Even in the low light, Portia could see the bloodied knuckles from where he'd beaten his porter.

"I suppose you're the reason this little rat was out of her nest, scurrying about the halls like vermin?" He shoved Maisie further into the hallway, and a whimper escaped her throat, though Portia wasn't sure where the noise had come from.

The dear girl had shown such courage amidst

the gloom of their circumstances. Portia had entrusted her with a task, and she had sent her headlong into danger.

His grin widened, "Cat got your tongue, Portia?"

"Let her go."

"Come now," he intoned casually as if they were sitting down to a meal, "what kind of fool do you take me for?"

"The last thing I would call you is a fool, Mr Finnegan." She could see bruises forming on Maisie's face already as he began to move backwards along the hallway, though William had fresh scratches on his arms. *Good.* That meant Maisie still had some fight left in her, even though her big tear-filled eyes were silently pleading with Portia. She couldn't look at her charge. She had to stay focused. She followed William down the corridor. "Please, don't hurt her."

"You know," he mocked her as he moved. "I had high hopes for you, Portia. Someone who looks as good as you do… I would have been happy to take you as a wife if it wasn't for your intrusion on issues that didn't concern you."

"Wouldn't I have a say in that?"

He laughed then. "I can be charming when I want to be. It worked with the late Mrs Finnegan. She didn't look as good as you do, but she was a warm body. Too bad that her feminine curiosity got the better of her. She had to go."

"You killed her."

He tutted, pausing in his movements. He cocked his head, and lowered his voice, "The official story is that she fell down the stairs, Portia. It was a thrill knowing that I was burying offcuts of random bodies in her coffin though. It was the only time in her life that that woman became useful."

He winked at her. Her instincts were telling her to run, to get help, but he knew fine and rightly that she wouldn't leave Maisie behind. And as her eyes met Finnegan's, the terrible realisation hit her —he wouldn't be admitting any of this if he thought she was getting out of here alive.

"Maisie hasn't done anything wrong. Can you let her go?"

He was on the move again. "Now, why would I do such a thing?"

"I'm the one you want, Billy."

Using his first name had unsettled him. His brows crunched together, and she held her ground as his eyes meandered down her form.

It was now or never.

"I can keep a secret, too. I've kept one ever since I got here. My name isn't Portia Summerhill, It's Lydia. Lydia Foxhall." She watched him carefully, waiting for recognition.

"What?"

"I was an inmate here, Mr Finnegan. I was just a girl."

Eyes narrowed, he said, "You were collected. You had an...aunt if I remember correctly. Last time I checked, you'd both emigrated. Your aunt died."

There was an uptick at the edges of her mouth. Rosamund had explained that she needed a change of scenery, though Portia now knew better. Her aunt wanted to end the trail in case someone ever came looking for her niece. "More of an extended holiday but yes, my aunt passed away. That was when I found the paperwork. Thankfully, my aunt was a determined woman. She was also fastidious in her paperwork. I'm certain you could have learned a thing or two from her.

I found the letters from my aunt, and the other workhouse establishments between here and where my mother's last letter to her had said we were. As soon as I saw them, all the memories I'd locked away in the back of my mind came flooding back.

I'd been told that my mother had abandoned me at the doors, but I remembered being in the porter's office..." Her gaze dropped to Maisie's open-eyed stare. *Just like you*, she wanted to say. She couldn't afford to be distracted, not yet. "I came back under an assumed name. John told me everything. Let her go, Billy. I'm the one that can bring down your empire."

He yanked Maisie off her feet and carried her the last few feet, tossing her in through an open doorway. Maisie grunted as she hit the stone floor. Too late, Portia recognised the narrow doorway, concealed in the stone wall. A cry ripped from her throat as she launched herself at William Finnegan. But he was ready for her. Pain seared into her side as she remembered the knife in his hand. She cried out and pressed a hand to where it burned. She saw the blood smeared across her palm.

She raised her eyes to his, and his delighted cackle filled her ears. With a shove, he sent her tumbling in through the door behind Maisie.

CHAPTER 27

*I*n the inky blackness of the cellar, Portia felt the weight of the air push against her. The thudding sound of several locks slid into place, sealing them inside. Her heart raced, an icy chill seeping into her bones. A terror she'd never known anchored her feet to the ground.

Beside her, Maisie's voice quivered, "Is everything you said true?"

"Yes."

"What happened to my mother?" Maisie sounded so uncertain, like a small child.

She instinctively reached out, wrapping her arms around Maisie, and pulling her close. The guilt pressed down on her, a stifling weight, knowing she was the reason Maisie was caught in this hellish predicament.

"I'm so sorry," she whispered, her voice barely audible. "I got you into this mess."

"Please, I have to know what happened."

Even now, locked inside, their doom sealed, Portia couldn't bring herself to say the words out loud. That being in this room would have been how both of their mothers likely met their deaths.

"Don't think about that," she whispered instead.

"What is this place? What is going to happen, Miss Summerhill?"

Summerhill. Her mother's maiden name. She'd chosen it as an act of defiance.

All Portia could hear, apart from the frantic beat of her own heart, was the ominous clanking and bubbling of pipes embedded in the thick walls around them. Finnegan had lit the fire.

The silence was interrupted by an overpowering, foul odour that permeated the air — the unmistakable stench of rotten eggs.

Coal gas.

"What is that *smell*?"

Portia's mind raced as the stink invaded her nostrils. She tried to cover her nose, her eyes watering. "Try to limit your breathing, Maisie." She recalled a passing comment from John about a ventilation shaft in the cellar. A window where victims had shouted for help.

Help. Who could they shout to? Inmates were locked away.

Matron Pursley.

Was she in on it, too?

"Maisie!" she gasped, "There's a vent in here somewhere? Help me look for it."

Maisie wretched, hacking in the darkness. "Where? I can't see a bloody thing in here!"

In the consuming darkness, Portia's pupils strained, and suddenly, she detected the faintest glimmer — a minuscule crack, a source of fresh air. With newfound urgency, she lurched towards it, her movement hindered by the cloying blackness. Suddenly, she stumbled, crashing into something on the floor.

Groping around, she felt coarse fabric and a wooden frame, realising it was a makeshift cot. She climbed atop it, her fingers searching desperately for the vent, struggling for breath, "It's up here! Help me. Follow the sound of my voice!"

The toxic air seemed to thicken around her, making every breath a laborious task. The wound in her side screamed and there was an iron grip that tightened around her brain, while her heart-beats felt muffled, as though submerged in thick syrup. Her legs felt as if they were encased in lead, but she forced herself to remain upright, desperate fingers that weren't cooperating scrambling against the wood. Splinters stabbed her fingertips and stars danced in her vision. For a moment, she teetered at the edge of blackness. Light exploded in her head as the vent slid open, shrill sounds filling her mind.

The shrieking got louder still, blaring all around.

Then she was tumbling, falling, her arms wheeling, as she landed. But there was no pain, only fuzzy cotton. She held her hands out to the warm smiling face waiting there for her. Laughter dancing in those eyes, so like her own. Happiness blooming.

She had found her mother.

CHAPTER 28

*C*onfusion.

More than once, Portia had clawed her way up through the confounding wool, only to slide back down. Unfamiliar noises. Voices that she didn't recognise. Foreign smells that burned. Pain. Then nothing.

Until she opened her eyes. Instead of darkness, there was cerulean blue – the kind that gave a cool crisp morning on a winter's day. A long window. Whitewashed walls.

She blinked, frowning, her mouth dry. Pain lanced down her left side. She searched around her, not recognising anything.

Except for the dark-haired man sleeping in the chair next to her bed. She blinked groggily. When she tried to speak, she emitted a croak. In the stillness of the room, it was enough of a sound to jolt him awake.

"Lydia?" Theo's feet struck the floor as he rose, concern creasing his brow. Deep green eyes searched her face, and he gently laid a hand on hers. "Darling, Lydia."

"Where am I?"

He lifted her hand to his mouth, lightly brushing the back of her hand with his lips. "My darling, you're in a hospital," he murmured. Seeing her frown deepening as she tried to dredge up memories from the depths of her mind, he continued, "Let me fetch the doctor. Try to stay awake a little longer this time, if you can." Tenderly, he pressed a kiss to her forehead before leaving the room.

Beyond the door, she heard voices and footsteps, growing louder until Theo returned, accompanied by a man in a white overcoat and a nurse trailing closely.

"Hello, I am Doctor Hart," the man said with a brisk tone that spoke of efficiency. "How are you feeling?"

Portia's eyes travelled around the room. "Muddled," she admitted honestly. "How did I get here?"

The trio exchanged glances, each more weighted than the last.

The doctor leaned over her, staring into one eye and then the other. "Do you remember anything?"

Closing her eyes, a kaleidoscope of images danced behind her lids. Her eyes snapped open. "Brookford. I was at Brookford."

The doctor's face relaxed into a slight smile. "Well done. That's significant progress."

Portia's eyes sought Theo, and she reached out a hand to him. "Please explain why I'm here."

As the doctor carried out a brief examination on Portia, Theo began, "You were in a small room, almost like a cellar."

Suddenly, the noise outside the door intensified. Maisie burst into the room, a striking change from her last appearance with her clean face framed by curly hair and wearing a simple blue shift dress. In a heartbeat, the dam in Portia's mind broke.

Recollections of Maisie crying, of being trapped in darkness, of choking on poisoned air, came rushing back to Portia.

"You can't be in here," a nurse protested as other familiar faces, Doris and Agatha, followed by Matron Pursley, appeared in her room.

"It's fine," Portia asserted, her voice gaining strength amidst the din of the protesting newcomers. "They can come in."

"Miss Foxhall," Doctor Hart interjected firmly.

"You can't put undue stress on yourself. You suffered carbonic oxide poisoning."

"*What* kind of poisoning?" Portia's voice was sharp, her memory gradually piecing together.

Theo, seeing her distress, gently nudged the doctor back. "Darling, you've been in this hospital for nearly two weeks. The doctors have been treating the carbonic oxide poisoning with oxygen in a hyperbaric chamber.

You've been in and out of consciousness, even experiencing fits. Only in the last few days have you shown significant improvement. You've spoken a few times, but it's been mostly gibberish. Please, don't strain yourself."

"I remember," Portia whispered, her gaze travelling around the room, "I remember what happened. I just don't know how I got here."

"From what I've been able to piece together," Theo began slowly, "young Miss Milne over there isn't particularly adept at following instructions." A titter of laughter moved through the room.

"Thank the Lord for small mercies," Agatha exclaimed.

"Yes, indeed," Theo responded with a smile. "Before she was discovered and taken by the master, Miss Milne had opened both dormitories and awakened several of the inmates, dispatching them quickly and quietly to the local village to raise the alarm. Matron Pursley played a crucial role, guiding the others out the back of the building to ensure they remained undetected."

"Just as you dropped like a sack of spuds, the police were running up the drive, blowing whistles and waving truncheons," Maisie interjected.

"Pandemonium ensued," Matron muttered, "but we prevailed."

"William Finnegan screamed and cussed like a banshee when the three officers restrained him, waiting for the wagon to cart him away," Maisie added with a hint of pride.

"The doctor mentioned that because you're taller, you felt the effects of the gas more rapidly," Theo noted. "But the fact that you knew about the window and got it open when you did mean that the worst effects of the gas were avoided."

"You saved me," Maisie told her.

"You saved us all, by the sounds of it, Maisie."

"And now that we've caught you up on every-thing," Doctor Hart remarked, "I must insist that you rest, Miss Foxhall. Your body has undergone a significant ordeal."

"I am rather tired," Portia admitted. "But just one more question before you all go, please."

"Very well," Doctor Hart relented.

"Where is the workhouse master?"

"Where his kind belongs," Agatha stated, though

she was promptly hushed by the matron. "Don't you be shushing me after what he's done," Agatha huffed and folded her arms. Matron Pursley didn't argue any further.

"Mr Finnegan is in Strangeways prison, awaiting trial for his crimes," Theo declared, his voice edged with a hint of steel. He gently laid a palm to Lydia's cheek, and she leaned into his touch. "He can't hurt you or anyone else anymore. Even if he escapes the hangman's noose, I'm certain the testimonies of all the inmates who suffered under his rule will ensure he never breathes fresh air as a free man ever again."

"He killed my mother," Lydia whispered thickly, tears spilling through her lashes. "Maisie's, too. And countless others, Theo."

"You will get to tell your story, Lydia. You will. But you must now rest. Get better. And then you can come home to me."

Lydia linked her fingers through his and held on a little longer. The room grew quieter, and she nodded at Maisie before the young girl disappeared through the door. Only then did she allow the tears to come. She wept. She'd come to Brookford to find answers about what happened to her mother. Ever since her aunt's death, and the reading of the will when her past had begun to come to light, the plan to go back to the workhouse where it had all started had been her primary objective.

The doctor slipped from the room and Theo pressed kisses to her head, her temple.

Now, in the aftermath, she knew. Her mother had been murdered. Her brother sold. But that knowledge didn't bring her the comfort she dreamed of. She'd wanted the love of a mother, to lay the ghosts of the past to rest.

She wept for all that she had lost, for all that she had discovered.

"My darling," Theo held her as the storm of emotions shook her. "The fight isn't over yet, but you are through the worst of it."

"I am a daughter of the workhouse, Theo. Your mother will never allow your family name to be dragged through the mud of a murder trial."

"My mother knows it all, Lydia," Theo chuckled wryly. "The newspapers have run with the story. I believe it's even made the papers across the Atlantic. More and more families are coming forth every day, whose family members vanished.

I would say she's happy that her son's choice of wife has brought about the end of a prolific murderer," he settled himself on the bed next to her, her head in the crook of his arm and added drolly, "She will be dining on this news for years to come."

In all the tumultuous emotions, she couldn't stop the laugh that huffed out. "Theo... you really shouldn't make jokes at a time like this."

"Darling, if we can't laugh when the world is falling apart around us, then when can we?" He rubbed his lips to her crown. "If I'd had a clue what was really going on in that place, I never would have left you there."

"I didn't tell you because I didn't know, not really."

His sigh filled the room. "I wanted to be the one to save you. Instead, you saved yourself and everyone in that place."

She leaned into him, the remnants of a smile quivering at the edges of her mouth. "But now I don't know what to do with myself."

"You can start by finally agreeing to be my wife."

She toyed with the chain of his pocket watch as she contemplated what she would do now. Part of her wanted the anonymity of becoming Mrs Theodore Whittonstall and yet... faces of inmates swam in her mind.

"But, knowing you," he murmured, "you'll not be content with just that. We'll figure it all out, though, won't we, my darling?"

"Yes," she whispered, as a piece of her heart clicked into place. "I do believe that we will."

trangeways Prison,
Manchester

CONNIE BARROW PULLED her shawl tighter around her shoulders as she stepped through the impressive prison gates sandwiched between the gatehouses. The minaret-like chimney stood out of the city skyline as a beacon, warning the city folk of the criminals that lurked within the walls of Strangeways prison.

The atmosphere inside was dank and dismal, the damp walls oozing with decades of despair. Guards eyed her with a mixture of disdain and bored curiosity, their eyes lingering on her just a moment too long, their comments whispered but audible. Connie questioned her decision to come here today, longing for the rolling green hills of home.

"This way," a surly guard barked, leading her down a corridor. His boots thudded heavily against the stone floor, and she was reminded of another place, of being locked in, long ago.

She had to remind herself that she'd escaped there. That she'd not looked back on the workhouse life, nor Brookford, not once. A fact that she was very proud of. Yet, each time a door clanged shut behind her, it amplified Connie's feeling of entrapment. Each door they passed seemed to clang shut with a finality that shook her to her core.

Finally, they arrived at a small room.

"Wait there," the prison office jabbed toward the one wall. The upper portion held a wire grating, through which she spotted another guard seated. She tiptoed closer. The channel he sat in was around four feet wide. Directly opposite where she stood was another aperture, identical to the one she stood in front of. The seated guard gestured for her to sit, and she took a place on the hard, wooden bench. Beyond the caged window, the sky was ominously grey. The rain that had been threatening throughout her train ride here fell in curtains.

Moments later, another door clanged open, and

a rattling chain and footsteps approached.

When William Finnegan stepped up to the iron bars opposite hers, his eyes met Connie's with an initial expression of puzzlement. She held the gaze, studying the face before her, taking in the changes as his face shifted to one of utter astonishment.

"Connie?" he finally managed to splutter; his voice tinged with disbelief.

He was older, his features hardened by years and circumstance, but the vestiges of the boy she once knew lingered in his dark eyes. The contours of his face, the curve of his jaw, were unmistakably that of the boy she once knew. He was still handsome, in a rugged, weathered way. Light caught in the silver at his temples.

"Yes, Billy, it's me," she finally said.

"You came." His astonishment had not yet abated.

The silence that followed was heavy, laden with years of memories and unspoken words. She found it difficult to reconcile this man, caged and worn, accused of dreadful, terrible deeds, with the charming, carefree youth she had once adored. He'd once stepped in front of a monstrous workhouse master to save her. Yet, here he was, a man clad in prison garb, his wrists chafed by iron shackles.

"Billy," she whispered, trying in vain to steady her voice. "Oh, Billy."

He hung his head, his face darkening. "Don't, Connie. Please."

"Why did you write to me then?"

He took his time in answering her. "I never believed you would come. Not for a minute. Everyone has turned their back on me. The Reverend has cut me out of his life, like the cancer that I am.

John Cobb upped and died, but not before he saw to it that I took the blame for everything," he added bitterly. Connie wanted to contradict him. A statement from the Brookford board of Guardians in one of the papers she'd seen had painted both men as bad and as guilty as the other. "After the conviction came, I wanted to say goodbye to you."

The letter had been tucked away in a bundle. It had been the last thing she'd opened that day. She hadn't recognised the neat writing on the front. Reading the heartfelt contents had brought her to tears.

"I didn't believe it all, not at first," she said. "I saw the newspapers and I thought to myself, not my Billy. Not the boy who grew up at Brookford. Not my Billy who saved me from the evil work-house master, Edward Trott."

A humourless laugh pierced the air. When he met her gaze, she caught the malicious gleam in them. She got a glimpse of the darkness that lived within him. "That's just it. I was never *your* Billy, was I? You chose Oscar over me. Maybe if you had, I wouldn't be here."

Connie blinked, her spine stiffening with indignation. "It was always Oscar, Billy. You know that. I loved him from the first moment I met him."

"Where is he now? Saint bloody Oscar, letting his wife into a hellhole like this," Billy threw his hands up as far as the iron chains would allow. "Didn't he want to face his old friend?"

"He passed away last spring, Billy. I'm a widow."

His hands dropped. The hardness in his eyes had softened, replaced by a glimmer of the vulnerability that she once knew so well. "I–I'm sorry. I didn't know."

The weight of their shared history hung in the air, a ghostly presence in a room already haunted by so many lost souls.

"We have two sons and a girl. Our eldest boy, William, is at university. He won a scholarship."

"You…you named your child William?"

"Billy," she corrected in a whisper. "After the man who once saved me."

For a moment, he looked away, his eyes perhaps chasing memories down some distant corridor of his mind. When he looked back at her, she saw sadness there. "That man vanished a long time ago."

Tears fell unchecked down her cheeks. "Billy,

did you do what the papers say? Did you... Did you kill those people?"

His throat worked as he swallowed. He nodded, reluctantly.

"Why? We were both so proud of you when we heard that you'd become a master at Brookford. I wanted to visit but Oscar... he couldn't be in enclosed spaces afterwards, let alone step through those doors again. He believed it to be a bad omen. I checked in now and again, then I heard you'd married, and were happy."

"Everything I wanted people to think," he muttered. "Everything I believed I needed to be to make Reverend James happy, but deep down, I was always that poor boy who wasn't ever good enough.

I studied, just as he wanted. It was never enough. Ambition was replaced by greed and the desire to never be in a position where someone could rule over me. Do you understand?"

She thought about the simple farmhouse in which she'd built a life with Oscar. They'd happily rented it throughout the years. How hard she'd worked to bring in extra funds during the leaner winter months. That both she and her wonderful husband ensured that the children could read and could write, so as not to find themselves facing the workhouse gates ever again.

She shook her head. "No. We had each other. We had food in our bellies. A roof over the heads of our children. We were warm in the winter months. For us, that was enough."

She knew she'd said the wrong thing when his gaze closed off, replaced by the hard façade of a man she didn't recognise. "You did choose right in the end, Connie. I would never have made you happy either." He rapped the iron bars in front of him, turning away from her. "I'm ready to go back now."

"Billy, wait!"

He paused, facing away from her, his head cocked back to listen.

"We won't meet again," Connie said gently. "I know that somewhere deep inside, you're a good man. That you regret what you did."

William Finnegan shook his head though didn't meet her eyes. He held his hands out to the guard, the rattle of chains ominous. "No, I'm not a good man. I lived a fine life and earned more coin than I ever could as an honest man. The truth is, Connie, I had my chance at a good life.

I didn't hesitate when I found a way to make more money dishonestly. I'd probably do it all again. If you'd have chosen me, I'd have taken you down with me. You picked the better man.

Goodbye, Connie."

EPILOGUE

*M*aisie's boots crunched on the icy gravel as she hurried along the long driveway of Willow Grange. Her breath clouded in front of her in the chilly air. Overhead, the bare branches of ancient oaks sparkled with a fresh coating of frost, as though touched by winter's magic. The rolling Shropshire hills were a distant backdrop, draped in a silvery mist.

Through a stand of evergreens, the grand house itself began to come into view—its golden bricks glowing in the nascent sunlight.

She stopped to adjust the basket on her arm. It was heavy, laden with fresh bread that tantalised the senses, and jars filled with delights that would be whipped into magnificent feasts for tonight's meal, no doubt.

Maisie had never tasted food as wonderful as the meals she'd eaten in the servant's hall. She gobbled up each and every morsel without fail, though she had drawn the line at the slimy oysters they'd been served that one time.

She hurried along, mindful of the time, when she still had so much to do. She wasn't sure why she'd been tasked with the errand into the village. Usually, the hallboy or one of the other maids would go. Not that she minded. The invigorating chill of the morning and the privilege of being out in nature made her thankful for the deviation in routine. With the rising sun burning off the morning haze, and the skeletal trees emerging, stretching their arms towards the sky ablaze with colour, it was a painter's morning.

Cattle lowed gently from the field that bordered the meandering drive, and sheep lazily spotted the distant pastures.

She ducked under the ivy-covered arch around the side of the house. As she reached the back entrance of Willow Grange, she kicked off the mulch clinging to her boots and pushed through the kitchen door, mindful of the scalding that she would invoke by one of the staff if she traipsed it all through the house. She stepped into the bustling cordiality of the kitchen and was immediately enveloped in the warmth. The rich aroma of roasting meats wafted through the air, tantalizing her senses. Despite a hearty breakfast of fresh farm eggs and a crusty roll, her stomach growled in anticipation.

Mrs Seddon, the cook, glanced up from her stovetop duties. "Ah, there you are," she said, wiping her hands on her apron. Her tone was brisk, but Maisie had not known a moment of cruelty from the kindly woman. "Quick as you can, leave those there. Alice will see to them."

Maisie set down the basket on a nearby table. "You're wanted upstairs."

Maisie felt a twinge of apprehension. She shucked off her coat and bonnet, hanging it on a hook by the door. She slipped her apron over her head. "Am I in trouble?"

"Maisie!" The housekeeper, Mrs Robson, trotted by. "You're back. No apron, my dear. She's waiting for you upstairs. In the library."

Of course, Maisie remembered. *No aprons above stairs.* So many rules to learn in service, though it was a career to be proud of. Every staff member was happy to be employed at such a grand house as this. Maise returned her apron to the long peg board on the wall.

"Did I do something wrong?" She asked the housekeeper, but she was already halfway along the narrow corridor and heading for her pantry. Maisie still hesitated.

"Not that I know of," Mrs Seddon replied, her attention already returning to the sauce she was stirring on the stove. "Off you go then. Don't dawdle."

Confused but intrigued, Maisie made her way to the back staircase. She knew the house, of course. In her daily tasks as a maid, she moved freely around the house, cleaning and working as part of a team of staff. She was allowed a half day off, with extra time if she requested it, not that she had anywhere else to go. But still, sometimes just to be able to walk outside without hearing a lock sliding home behind her was magical in itself.

The door at the top of the narrow staircase opened into the wide foyer. Crowned with an elaborate chandelier, winter sun streamed through the towering windows framed by heavy damask curtains. The effect was a cascade of golden sunbeams that scattered across the polished parquet floors, creating an enchanting interplay of light and shadow.

Large porcelain vases filled with winter blooms stood proudly on marble tables, filling the air with a subtle floral fragrance that mingled with the beeswax from the polished furniture.

The elegant staircase swept up to the first floor,

spreading its intricately carved balusters and handrails like arms to encompass the gallery. The stairs were carpeted with a lush, ruby-red runner that contrasted dramatically against the gleaming dark wood. Her footfall was muffled by the ornate oriental rugs underfoot.

She proceeded through a side doorway, too nervous to enter the grand library through the main door. She was greeted by the rich aroma of aged leather and parchment. Bookshelves reached nearly to the ceiling, each carrying an assortment of tomes, their spines showcased a myriad of colours, with gold leaf titles hinting at the wisdom they contained. A towering globe stood in one corner, inviting exploration of its own, and artworks depicting landscapes and historical events adorned the walls.

A massive, Persian rug sprawled beneath her feet, softening her steps, and adding warmth to the room. At the far end, a wide hearth roared with a fire, the flames dancing shades of orange and yellow, suffusing the room with a warm, welcoming glow. Above the fireplace hung an oil painting of the original owner, stern-faced but kindly-eyed, as if watching over the generations who sought comfort and knowledge in this very room.

Comfortable leather chairs and sofas were scattered about, some drawn close to the fireplace for warmth. A few tables, inlaid with intricate patterns, held current reading materials and ornate oil lamps.

A plush, emerald-green armchair sat invitingly close to the fire, accompanied by a small side table that held a crystal decanter filled with what appeared to be fine Scotch. It was the occupant of the chair that Maisie focused on.

"Oh, my dear," Mrs Draper's hands fluttered, beckoning or halting, Maisie couldn't tell.

The older woman had been a firecracker in the aftermath of what had happened at Brookford. She might look as if a strong wind would despatch her, but Maisie knew that the older woman had a granite core.

"Come, come," she popped up, fiddling with her hair. "Please, there's someone who wants to see you."

Maisie stepped further into the room and that's when she saw the other occupants in the room. Lydia and her new husband, Theo Whittonstall, seated on a mustard-coloured two-seater sofa. Maisie couldn't help the beaming smile as she stepped towards the woman who'd saved them all though it was the movement at her periphery that stopped her heart. Framed by the light streaming through the narrow window he was stood in front of.

For just a moment, she thought that maybe she was dreaming again. After all, that swaggering smile and twinkling blue eyes shimmered in her visions each night.

The air in the room felt thick and she swung back to the others, only this time they didn't morph into black eyes devils, with roving hands. She latched onto Lydia's warm gaze, who nodded at her.

She looked back at the young man who was nervously threading his cap through his fingers. His hair was shorter. His clothing was different. But he was very much alive.

"D-Duncan?" The name was unfamiliar as it left her lips. She hadn't been able to think about him, instead focusing on finding her feet in her new role after Mrs Draper had agreed to take her in. Maisie had once hoped that she could go with Lydia and Mr Whittonstall, but they'd whisked off to get married and deal with the legal side of the trial.

"Hello, Maisie," his mouth was propped up on one side and her heart lurched, his voice like a balm to the void in her that his disappearance had left.

"You're...real?"

Laughter shone in his beautiful blue eyes. "Yes, my love."

"But... how? We all thought... I thought...you were..." Her mind stumbled, and she tried to grab onto one coherent word.

Lydia appeared at her side, a reassuring hand in the middle of her back, rubbing her. "Before he died, John Cobb told me that Duncan hadn't ever been in the deadhouse. Why don't you tell her the rest, Duncan?"

He bobbed his head in gratitude. "Thank you, Mrs Whittonstall. You remember that day I stepped under Matron's cane?"

Maisie nodded. The proceedings of that day were emblazoned in her mind. She'd relived them over and over again, more so since she'd left Brookford.

"I got tossed into the cold room for it," Duncan said, and Mrs Draper made a little sound of distress. Even now, months after everything had settled, even after everything she'd heard about the goings-on at the workhouse, Maisie knew it filled the compassionate older woman with horror. "In the hubbub of what was happening in those last few days, whether or not Cobb had his mind else-where, he didn't lock the door. I slipped away intending to come back for you.

I went back to the farmhouse I used to live in with my family. I'd hid some of my parents' clothing in the barn. I remember people who'd escaped in the past had always been found because of what they'd worn. I don't know why I did it... but I suppose it served me right and I wasn't found.

I had to find some work, to be able to buy a mangle, just as we planned. I went north to Liverpool and found work at the docks there. I figured just a couple of weeks wouldn't do any harm. That if you went to The River Maiden, I knew where to find you.

Then I saw that I was too late. It was all in the newspapers. I wondered if you'd been amongst the victims, but no one could tell me. All the inmates scattered to the winds.

I came back and no one would tell me anything. The interim Master thought I was a man trying to dig into the sordid details so that I could sell more newspapers. It turns out that Mrs Whittonstall was just protecting you. She'd been the one to keep your name out of everything, even though she tells me you were the one who'd let everyone out that night and sent them to get help from the town."

"He was persistent, Maisie," Lydia said softly. "He kept going back. He annoyed the new workhouse master enough times that he happened to mention it to Doctor Jenkins. He remembered you. He knew that I was looking for Duncan."

"You were?"

"Yes," Lydia's eyes shone. "That's where I've

been for the past few months. Not just trying to find him, of course, but making sure that all the inmates were settled and cared for. Looking for my brother, too."

Duncan stepped a little closer to her, his head tilting as he caught her tears shining in the sunlight on the tip of his thumb. "To my eternal shame, Maisie, I ran. I would have stayed if I had known what was going to happen. I tried to find you but... in my mind, I knew I had nothing to offer you. We'd have probably ended up right back in the workhouse. But I should have tried harder."

"I don't care about all of that," she whispered. "You're alive. You're safe. That's more than I could have wished."

"I told you that she'd say that, old chap," Theo chuckled.

Duncan's smile grew. "Not quite like walking over hot coals to get to you, but I never gave up hope."

"You're here," Maisie cried, and fell into his embrace, rejoicing in the sensation of being wrapped up in his arms. All the lonely nights, the pain and the tears...none of it seemed to matter now.

"Yes, my heart, I'm here."

"Goodness," Mrs Draped sniffed, dabbing delicately at her eyes. "And that's not all the news that

Mrs Whittonstall and her husband bring here today, either."

Maisie turned in the embrace to look back at her employer. "What do you mean?"

Lydia glanced at Theo, a smile playing on her mouth. Theo laid an arm around her shoulders and grinned at Maisie. "She's talked of nothing but you for months. Telling me how brilliant you are. How bright, clever... resourceful," he added with a chuckle.

"We've come to take you home, Maisie. If you want to come that is," Lydia added.

Maisie's eyes wavered between them and looked up at Duncan. "I don't understand."

"Well, Mrs Draper has been kind enough to offer you refuge here. I gather her staff have looked after you well?"

"Oh, yes," Maisie nodded. "Everyone has been most welcoming and kind."

"Good, I'm so very glad to hear that," Lydia said. "Though the plan always was that once I'd dealt with the trial, and the inmates, and then Theo and I had settled in my aunt's home, you would come and live there with us."

Maisie's breath caught. She'd believed that Lydia had simply distanced herself from the whole debacle. When it had emerged that she was from a wealthy shipping family, and how she'd found her way back to them through her determined aunt after being an inmate, Maisie had accepted that her Miss Summerhill had her own life to lead, just as she did.

"What about your brother?" Maisie asked Lydia. "Have you found him?"

Theo shuffled closer to Lydia as she shook her head. "Not yet. The trial brought up many stories from the past though. There are lots of lines of enquiry for us to follow."

"We're not giving up, are we, my dearest one?" Theo brought Lydia's hand up to his mouth.

"Most definitely not," she whispered.

"I believe he's out there," Maisie offered.

A smile wobbled across Lydia's mouth. "Me, too."

"But do you need a servant? You don't need to do this – you've done enough."

Lydia laughed then, leaning into her husband's embrace. "Miss Milne, you have an exam to sit, remember?"

"And our new tenant could do with some help with his accounting," Theo quipped, sending a pointed look at Duncan.

She turned to Duncan. "You're the new tenant?"

"Yes, I am. They have a beautiful farm. Pigs and cattle. Some wheat fields. And I could do with more than a hand," Duncan cuddled her close. "I need you. I need a wife."

Theo laughed then. "Steady on, old chap. One step at a time."

"What do you say, Maisie?" Lydia asked her.

Maisie met their gazes, full of hopeful potential. "But what about Mrs Draper? She was kind enough to take me in, give me a chance?"

"Goodness, Maisie, you do not need to worry. I'm just so grateful that I saw some good come from the awful event. With Lydia's help, I've been able to help the children left behind at Brookford. We have a new system at the workhouse, with a closer hand on the records," Mrs Draper fluttered across her Venetian rug and pulled the cord that activated the bell down in the servant's hall. "I think this news calls for a celebration because, of course, you're going to accept such a wonderful offer. I shall ring for some tea, and we can all make a plan together."

AUTHORS NOTE

'Tis strange—but true; for truth is always strange,
Stranger than fiction: If It Could Be Told,

~ Don Juan, by Lord Bryon, 1823

This is a work of fiction but as with many of my stories, they are cemented in things I've read during researching a book.

Like many authors, I have a wild imagination. Yet sometimes real life is much more bizarre than fiction or anything I could create in my mind. I knew that I wanted to write a story set in a workhouse for my next book. Whilst researching (a.k.a dragging my ever-patient husband around dusty old museums and houses) I kept reading about the dreadful conditions of the workhouses, and the

Masters who ran them - and sometimes how they exploited the system for their own financial gains, including criminal activity. People lived in these buildings…and off goes my creative ideation, thinking about their lives and the stories that they would tell.

Brookford is a name I made up specifically for this book, but there are a few place names that are real.

Many smaller parishes in England used one form of workhouse or another as a way of managing the poor within the parish, and Shropshire was no different. These buildings still stand - though today, from the outside, they look a little more like grand homes.

The early 1800s saw several changes within the medical field. We began to understand just how important surgery was and that to grow our knowledge, we needed human bodies, and not animals, which medical students had been used to practising their skills on up until that time. For a while, hospitals were able to claim the bodies of criminals who'd been condemned to death. After all, no one can 'own' a dead body. But then the demand outstripped the supply - and we ended up with a 'grave' dilemma!

That's where the body snatchers - namely the Resurrectionists - began to meet that demand by exhuming freshly buried corpses and selling them to the medical and anatomy schools for a fee. Grave robbers could charge as much as £10 per body (Which, when you consider the average annual income in 1880 was £42 per year is a lot!) for each fresh adult corpse. There are famous cases whereby some individuals began to meet that demand by killing people instead of waiting for them to die.

Of course, work slowed down in winter but only because the ground was harder to dig into when frozen. Providing the Resurrectionists didn't steal any of the items that were buried in the caskets (jewellery items, like a wedding ring, for example) then they avoided criminal prosecution. Still, people didn't want their loved ones' bodies being stolen - and that's why you sometimes see cages over the tops of graves in the older graveyards.

Recognising the need for a solution, in 1832, the Anatomy Act was passed in the English Parliament. This act stated that doctors, surgeons, and medical students could have bodies, particularly those who died in workhouses or prisons if they hadn't been claimed by family members within a specified timeframe.

Considering the dire conditions in these institutions at the time, there was a ready supply for the hospital training schools. It was another reason why paupers feared the workhouse so much. They'd be buried in an unmarked grave or worse, sent to the anatomy school for parts.

However, between 1832 and 1844, medical professionals continued to exploit loopholes in the Act. Hospital schoolteachers often directed officials from workhouses and prisons, whose staff earned very little, to deliver the corpses to them, offering them £5 per body. Although the Anatomy Act did not specifically outlaw such sales, it soon became evident that the exchange of money for corpses was turning parish officials and workhouse staff into unscrupulous traffickers of dead bodies.

Another significant oversight in the Anatomy Act was its lack of stipulations regarding dismembered body parts. The Act only addressed whole corpses. This loophole in the law meant that medical schools could procure body parts without having to report this activity to the anatomy inspectorate, which governed this new law. This legislative oversight was a tad problematic, given that the statute intended to deter grave robbing and murder! Of course, it also meant that murder and grave robbing activities were particularly hard to detect when corpses were being sold in parts instead, raising concerns about the continuation of these activities post-1832.

Undertakers, despite being ideally positioned to provide corpses to medical schools due to their connections with parish networks and frequent presence in workhouses, were excluded from the Anatomy Act's purview. They were able to operate in the sales of dead bodies without control as the Act did not hold them accountable to the Anatomy Inspectorate.

The vulnerable populations within workhouses, many of whom were illiterate, were left at the mercy of officials who might exploit them.

Although the Anatomy Act was designed to control and regulate the use of corpses for medical purposes, its loopholes allowed for continued misuse. Even after the 1844 amendment to the Poor Law Act, banning workhouse masters from selling bodies, there were still instances for decades afterwards where workhouse masters continued to illicitly profit from supplying dead bodies to hospitals.

The Victorian era was a time of huge changes around the world. Coal gas had grown in popularity at the start of the 19th century as demand for fuels grew. It was highly flammable with a distinctly unpleasant smell of sulphur (smells like rotten eggs if you've ever been in a natural spring somewhere!) and was quickly replaced by natural gas, which was odourless.

It was piped into homes from iron gas stoves built by companies such as William Sugg & Co. in London.

We are lucky here in the UK to be surrounded by so much history. There are many workhouses still standing for you to be able to visit with records of these times painting the grimly macabre and rich tapestry of lives of days gone by.

Workhouses were formally ended in 1930, although did not disappear completely until 1948.

A.S.

PREQUEL TO THIS BOOK

Annie Shields lives in Shropshire with her husband and two daughters.

When she doesn't have her nose in a book, you'll find her exploring old buildings and following historical trails, dragging her ever-patient husband along with his trusty map.

If you would like to be amongst the first to hear when she releases a new book and free books by similar authors, you can join her mailing list HERE

As a thank you, you will receive a **FREE** copy of her eBook The Barefoot Workhouse Orphan - the prequel to this book, where we meet William Finnegan and Connie for the first time.

Your details won't be passed along to anyone else and you can unsubscribe at any time.

ALSO BY ANNIE SHIELDS

The Dockyard Darling

In the haunting aftermath of her father's sudden death, Ella Tomlinson finds herself at the mercy of her cruel stepmother, Clara. Desperate to escape a forced marriage, Ella seeks refuge with her estranged uncle in his lively tavern, hidden in the heart of London's bustling Docklands. Here, she is plunged into a dangerous world filled with sailors, boatmen, and shadowy traders. A world where she is safe until Clara finds where she is & tries to silence her forever.

The Queen of Thieves

Trixie White must learn to survive on the streets of Victorian London by all means necessary. But, working in a team of pickpockets, her quick hands and courage make her stand out. But when the Queen of Thieves is made to choose between the man that she loves or protecting her little sister, Trixie's battle takes a dangerous turn.

The Swindler's Daughter

After she discovers that her wealthy family are rotten to the core, Mollie Webster is cast out onto the streets of London. Frightened and alone, she must learn to trust her instincts in order to survive. But when Jack Taylor is thrust back into her life, can she truly believe that the only man she's ever loved isn't another thug sent by her family to destroy her?

Printed in Great Britain
by Amazon